WHAT REMAINS OF ELSIE JANE

a novel

WHAT REMAINS OF ELSIE JANE

a novel

Chelsea Wakelyn

Publisher: Kwame Scott Fraser | Acquiring editor: Russell Smith
Cover designer: Laura Boyle
Cover image: CSA-Printstock; Unsplash.com/Felix Mittermeier; Jeremy Thomas; Kiwihug; Andy Holmes

Library and Archives Canada Cataloguing in Publication

Title: What remains of Elsie Jane : a novel / Chelsea Wakelyn.
Names: Wakelyn, Chelsea, author.
Identifiers: Canadiana (print) 20220269254 | Canadiana (ebook) 20220269262 | ISBN 9781459750845 (softcover) | ISBN 9781459750852 (PDF) | ISBN 9781459750869 (EPUB)
Classification: LCC PS8645.A4535 W53 2023 | DDC C813/.6—dc23

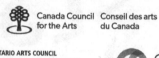

We acknowledge the support of the Canada Council for the Arts and the Ontario Arts Council for our publishing program. We also acknowledge the financial support of the Government of Ontario, through the Ontario Book Publishing Tax Credit and Ontario Creates, and the Government of Canada.

Rare Machines, an imprint of Dundurn Press
1382 Queen Street East
Toronto, Ontario, Canada M4L 1C9
dundurn.com, @dundurnpress 𝕏 f ⊙

For Kris

ONE

AT THE FUNERAL HOME, THEY GIVE ME WATER WITH lemon slices. It tastes like poison because everything tastes like poison now. They speak to me very softly, like I am a child about to go down for a nap, and they listen with their heads slightly tilted to demonstrate empathy. Ushered into a parlour with gilded floral wallpaper, I sit at a long, gleaming table of dark oak. It's a difficult time to make decisions, they tell me, and I think, *Thank God, they understand*. But then they give me a stack of papers to sign, which are full of decisions. Then come the catalogues of flowers and food menus to look at, also full of decisions. Sam's family and I look at these decision things as if they're written in hieroglyphics.

Another catalogue: pieces of jewellery that can be forged from ashes of the body. Unfortunately, I can't view the body right now, as it's being embalmed in the basement. But I don't want to see it, anyway, do I? If I see the body, that means the body is real.

"I don't want to see the body," I tell them.

"Well, you might change your mind," they say. "Many people find it a great comfort to see their loved ones at rest."

"Our mortician is excellent," they say. "Samuel will look just like he's sleeping."

Then they tell me to keep in mind that he'll be taken off-site for cremation by noon, so unfortunately there are some time constraints if I do decide to participate in the viewing.

"It's not him, though," I whisper.

No, darling, of course it's not me.

If Sam had known he was going to die at age forty-three, I bet he wouldn't have been upset about the white hairs sprouting from his chest and ears and back.

"Fuck, I hate getting old," he said one night as we drove the kids home from the pool.

"Why do you say that?"

"I don't know — just seeing my reflection in the change room. Don't you notice how much whiter my chest hair is, all of a sudden? It happened overnight."

"Growing older is a privilege."

"That's such a platitude. Growing old is entropy, and entropy is depressing."

"I love your white chest hairs. They make you look like a silverback gorilla. I'm going to lick every single one of them."

When we got home, he went into the bathroom and began plucking his back hairs with tweezers, inspecting his ears and trimming the sweet tufts of fur creeping out of them. I stood behind him and watched us both in the mirror. I made a duck face, then a monkey face. He swatted me away, so I kissed his shoulder blades.

"I love you," I said. "When I'm an old bird full of arthritis, will you pluck out all my white pubic hairs for me?"

"Of course I will. With my dentures, baby."

○

I do end up viewing the body. I'm the last to see it, and when I do, a howl rises up from the heart of the Earth, shoots up my legs into my guts and chest and up my throat, pours out of me in a flood of hot snakes.

The snakes come for a long time. Against the wall, then all over the floor. Every time I try to stop them, I catch a glimpse of Sam's face, and the room spins and the Earth sends up a fresh tsunami of pain.

At some point, my sister helps me up. I limp toward the body. He's so still, like he's just gotten dressed for a work meeting and fallen asleep. I run my fingers over his fingers, along the backs of his hands, under his suit jacket. I feel the autopsy staples running down his chest. He's in a T-shirt we bought during a trip to Tofino, a green one with antlers silkscreened on the front.

Please understand what a perfect face he has. It is the face that was made for my face, the face that kissed mine for hours and hours until my chin was raw and sore for days. Long black eyelashes, a strong and sculpted nose.

What happened? He went to sleep and he didn't wake up, that's all I know.

Please understand how beautiful he was.

○

Containers for bodies and ashes are a big deal, a critical source of revenue in the funeral industry. That's why the place where you pick out the containers looks like the showroom at a dealership, but with urns and caskets instead of cars.

I approach a shelf of urns. Some of them look like jewellery boxes, but they have framed pictures on the lids, featuring glamour shots of the happiest old people ever, smiling as big as they can, knowing they're going to get to spend eternity in a pewter box that's now 15 percent off.

There are also fancy ones with engraved plaques that say things like:

He gives His beloveds sleep ...

and

In God's care ...

and

Her wings were ready ...

"These are all terrible and ridiculous," I tell the funeral director.

"Oh, dear. Well, we can certainly go through the catalogue if you don't see anything to your liking."

What the managers of the industry of death don't want you to know, because they're on commission, is that you can put ashes in pretty much anything. I learned this when my dad died, and his wife went to Value Village and purchased a coffee canister for $6.99.

"My dad is in a coffee tin," I tell the director, "so I'm pretty sure Sam can go in any receptacle as long as it's sealable."

"Well, that is true. However, these products are designed specifically as keepsakes for remains, and they come with a guarantee."

"A guarantee for what?"

Everybody looks at me as if I just burst out laughing in a funeral parlour, because I did.

Thirty minutes later I am with Sam's family at the mall. We have come to the mall because it is a place with many stores, and we can all split up, which is obviously a more efficient way to locate an affordable sealable container for our loved one. I find myself in a fancy home-accessories store called Bombay Company. The saleswomen are dripping in gold, painted with orange foundation and caked blush. One of them is trying to be subtle about keeping an eye on me, which is very reasonable of her. I haven't slept in days and my face definitely has the puffy look of a shoplifter. I am also wearing sweatpants and a coffee-stained T-shirt that says *Obey Cthulhu.*

"Can I help you here, sweetheart?"

"Sure."

"Okay, what is it that I can help you with?"

"A container for my spouse's ashes. It has to be sealable."

She grimaces, tries to smile. I am examining a very lovely, extra-large jewellery box encrusted in fake sapphires with an elephant head on top.

"I like this one," I tell her, "but I think it might be too small. He was six foot one, so I don't know how much ashes he'll make. Also, do you have any that play music? Like T. Rex or Nick Cave?"

"Pardon me?"

My phone rings. It's Ingrid, Sam's sister.

"Come to HMV," she is shouting. "I've found the perfect thing. It's a fucking Death Star cookie jar — *come!*"

I tell the saleslady that my sister-in-law has found a Death Star cookie jar, which is perfect since my dead beloved was a Star Wars fan and our son was born on May the fourth.

"I might be back for this elephant one if the Death Star doesn't work," I tell her.

"Oh *my*," she says.

O

I have just submitted Sam's obituary. It isn't as good as it would have been if he hadn't just died, if I had slept for more than two hours, if I wasn't baffled and haunted and nursing a toddler.

Dead people are always presented as the most ideal versions of themselves. I know this from when my parents died. We want to feel peaceful in our rememberings. We want to feel like we are good people who ultimately see the best in others. Every flaw in the person is swiftly edited, every goodness amplified.

They weren't just generous, they were *munificent*.

They weren't just clever, they were *brilliant*.

It's fine to do this, to idealize our dead loves this way. Important, even. I've filled my boots with sunny, sanitized memories for hours at a time, but I've also learned that doing so makes the shitty visions of what stuff was *really* like more jarring when they come tumbling out of the slow-melting glaciers of your subconscious.

> Samuel Elias Sorensen
> November 7, 1972–December 7, 2015
> We are heartbroken to say goodbye to Sam, the most brilliant, gentle, generous man we've ever known.
> Born and raised in Calgary, Alberta, Sam excelled in school and was named "Most Likely to Discover a New Galaxy" in high

school. He won a scholarship to UC Berkeley, but ultimately chose to stay in Canada to be closer to family. Sam adored his family. He was a beloved mentor and tutor to many, including his younger cousins. In 1990, he moved to Victoria to attend UVic. After graduating with a B.Sc. in computer science with a minor in physics, he completed his M.Sc. in computer science in 2008. Sam's life ended unexpectedly while he was in the midst of earning his Ph.D., focusing on artificial intelligence and metacognition in computation. Sam's work would have changed the world.

He was a devoted, patient, playful father and stepfather to his kids, and was so looking forward to watching them grow up and continuing to share his love of Frisbee golf, philosophy, kites, music, sci-fi, comics, and mythology with them.

Sam is survived by his mother, Hannah Wilson (Tom); father, Magnus Sorenson (Lily); sister Ingrid (Arun); nephew Dev; son Quinn; spouse Elsie; son Benji; and stepdaughter Lark.

See?

TWO

TODAY IS FAMILY DAY, APPARENTLY, AND I AM GOING to a party. It's a street party.

"They're going to cordon off like ten blocks along the waterway. Come with us!" says my friend. "There will be face painting and food trucks and stuff!"

I can't imagine why anyone would think a street party in mid-February would be a good idea, but it's the weekend, and I have nothing else going on. Sam and I used to take the kids to visit his Danish grandfather, Mikkel, every Sunday. We'd bring him crusty buns, tomatoes, this stinky Danish cheese called esrom, and we'd sit around his table all afternoon while he aired each and every grievance of his life. Lark and Quinn would spin on the leather recliner, examine the ancient figurines in the curio cabinet.

Quinn has vanished from our daily lives, too. His mother moved back to Cape Breton to be closer to her parents the month after Sam died. Our little blended family of five is now separated by death and a continent. It's just me and Lark and Benji now. A mournful trio.

I've visited Mikkel once since the funeral, which was two months ago now. I did the same routine that Sam and I used to do: Maria's Deli to buy the buns and tomatoes and esrom, then wait at the gates of Mikkel's condo while he yelled, "*Who?!*" into the speaker fifteen times before giving up and pressing the buzzer to let in whoever we were.

I am a very kind and responsible granddaughter-in-law, I told myself as I cut the buns and arranged the tomatoes and cheese on the plate, but I regretted visiting Mikkel when he refused to move to the table or eat any of the food. He sat in his recliner, still in his pyjamas at one in the afternoon, weeping over a photo album of Sam as a child. It scared the shit out of Lark. She made herself small and curled up on the couch, staring wide-eyed at the cabinet of figurines as if seeing them for the first time. Mikkel tried coaxing Benji onto his lap, but he hid his face in my legs, which made the old man weep even more.

"Sam always loved to sit on my lap, you see? You see in this picture?"

O

Lark is at her dad's place this weekend, so I'm alone with Benji.

Weekends are hell. Long weekends are even worse, because I have to see everyone posting on Facebook about how much fun they're having with their intact families. Anyway, rather than spending a third afternoon in a daze watching Benji spin in circles in the living room, I'm actually leaving the house and going to this Family Day thing, even though I know it's probably going to be terrible because everything is terrible now.

I see Starla on my way out the door. Starla is the neighbour who lives in the other half of the duplex that Sam and I bought when I was pregnant with Benji. She's in her late fifties and wears shorts all year round. She has a Doberman, Sniper, who sits perfectly still and watches her vacuum out her truck every single day. We share a wall, so she probably hears me pacing and crying at night.

A couple of weeks after the funeral, she approached me, leaning over her side of the fence in the manner that every Concerned Gossip character loves.

"Sorry for your loss," she said.

"Thank you," I said.

"Aww," she said, making an exaggerated sad face. "It's hard, isn't it?"

"Yup."

"But you know ..."

Then she told me that even though she felt really sad about Sam being dead — don't get her wrong, it was terrible, *terrible!* — and even though she recognized the shape of mickeys in Sam's droopy pocket when he left for work in the mornings (and she could spot an alcoholic a mile away, on account of growing up with her asshole father who died of an enlarged heart, so young at only seventy-nine, so she knew how hard it was to lose someone), and even though she was sad, really sad, she wanted to tell me that she was also really glad it wasn't me who was dead. Because did I know that the very day Sam died, she had heard a report on the radio that the body of a female in her midthirties had been found in the bush behind the movie theatre a few miles away?

"No. Hadn't heard that."

Having seen the police cars in our driveway that day, Starla had Sherlocked it all out: Sam had murdered me and dumped my body behind SilverCity Cinema.

"Well, I'm still alive," I said. "Not murdered."

"What a coincidence, though, eh? Ha!"

"What a coincidence."

O

I immediately googled "body found SilverCity Cinema 2015," and found this:

> December 7, 2015
>
> SAANICH — Police are investigating a suspicious death after the body of a woman was found in Saanich's Cuthbert Holmes Park behind the SilverCity Cinema on Monday morning. Police cordoned off part of the park after the body was spotted in a marshy area by someone walking their dog, shortly before 8:30 a.m. Detectives and forensic investigators were on scene behind police tape throughout the morning. Police spokeswoman Sgt. Lauren Bain said the woman has not been identified, and the cause of her death is not yet known.
>
> "The coroner service is involved. They will be doing an autopsy. We won't speculate on her cause of death at this time," she said.
>
> Bain said police are still investigating and consider the death suspicious.
>
> "It's heartbreaking," Bain stated. "Anyone passing away in these circumstances, you know, it's just very sad."

By 11:45 a.m., the coroner had come
and gone, and the police tape was removed.
The park is now open to the public. Terry
Robertson lives in the area and said he walked
through the park at around 10:45 p.m. There
was no sign of the body at that time, he said.
He wondered if the woman might have been
homeless, as there is a group of homeless
people living in tents by the creek. Police
stated that they have not yet identified the
woman and have therefore been unable to
notify next of kin. Anyone with information
about the death is asked to contact Saanich
Police.

I mean, it *is* a coincidence, but let's be real: Sam could never
have murdered me. He really was the gentlest person I've ever
met, and I'm not just saying that. He was gentle in the same
way trees are gentle.

O

I've been ignoring Starla lately. I don't bother with fake polite-
ness anymore, and I can't stomach the thought of an exchange
with her, today especially. She's cleaning her truck, as usual.
Her butt-length ponytail swinging, her fanny pack of dog treats
hanging from her belly, her firm, tanned calves: all of these
things are upsetting. I pretend to examine my phone and rush
by her, but I hear the vacuum shut off and feel her eyes dig into
my back while I buckle Benji into his car seat. When I get into
the car, I make the mistake of glancing her way and find her

staring at me with the Shop-Vac hose slung over her shoulder, Sniper perched like a gargoyle behind her. I give her a *Fuck-you* thumbs-up. She frowns, turns the machine back on, goes back to sucking invisible dust.

Maybe I'll knock on her door tonight and let her know that if Sam actually wanted to murder me, he would have done a much more subtle and elegant job. He would have dissolved me in a bucket of chemicals and then poured me into a volcano, or pushed me off a cliff into an emerald lake, or slowly poisoned me with some undetectable toxin until my hair fell out and my bones crumbled.

O

"God*damn* it."

There is no parking anywhere near this block party. The closest spot I can find is over a mile away. Even better, I open the trunk to find that I've forgotten the stroller at home. There are dark clouds rolling in that look like rain. We are late meeting my friend, my phone is at 1 percent, and as I rush to compose a cancellation text, it dies.

This is fine. My insane toddler and I will just walk down this incredibly dangerous, narrow sidewalk as cars rush past, because we are going to have fun today. Fun on Family Day.

Somehow we make it to the street party without getting hit by a bus or a meteor.

There are vintage cars, jugglers, hot dogs. The air smells of cotton candy and burger meat and sweat. There are balloons and tiger stripes painted on children's faces. Who the fuck came up with Family Day, anyway? What a horrible idea for a day.

"I'm so glad I got you out of the house!" says my friend. Her husband gives me a noogie and a kiss on the cheek.

"Benji doesn't like it here," I say.

He has spent every moment since our arrival running into people's yards and pulling up their flowers. My friend keeps trying to chat with me, but I can't sustain conversation because I have to keep chasing and grabbing the kid before he mutilates another garden bed. Every time I pick him up, he arches his back, screaming and thrashing, but my friend keeps saying things to me and I just have to keep nodding and smiling and pretending to know what we're talking about.

I pry a geranium from Benji's fist, and he collapses in a tantrum.

My friend shrugs and smiles. "Don't worry about it," she says. "We've all been there."

"Have we?" I snap. "Have we *all* been here?"

This is the problem with being around people. I can't do it anymore. I can't pretend that I'm a normal human having a regular good time. I look at my friend, watch her face fall, and I don't even care if I'm making things awkward. She still has her husband, and I hate her for it. She must sense my hostility because she suddenly feels the need to go check on her own kids by the hot dog stand. She disappears into the crowd.

My kid is still on the ground, kicking and covering his ears. "Too loud! Too loud!" he's shrieking.

It *is* too loud. There is a band in a nearby driveway playing a Rush cover.

"Rush fucking sucks!" I yell at the sky.

A posh mom covers her daughter's ears and shakes her head at me.

I look around and realize that I'm standing in the middle of a river. It is a river of moms and dads and grandparents and kids — but mostly dads. Dads with little boys on their shoulders. So many of them. A river of them, parting around us but flowing nonetheless while I stand here, alone with my fatherless child who will never experience such a simple, stupid thing as a ride on his dad's shoulders at a street party. It occurs to me that maybe he senses this, too, our otherness here, and that's why he's crying.

I try to calm his angry limbs, gather him up.

If only I could jump universes. If only I could figure a way to climb out of this one.

I'm fat and exhausted in wool tights that are riding down so my thighs rub together. My ears are burning from the Rush cover and my eyes are burning from the smells and tears, and all I want is for some merciful deity to rip open the fabric of space-time, drop a ladder from the sky, and whisper, "Climb, my girl, climb! There's a beautiful black hole up here, waiting just for you!"

That's obviously not going to happen, so I buy a hot dog, drench it in mustard, and limp back to the car, scowling at strangers and eating from one hand while the other grips Benji to my hip.

"Don't cry, Mama."

"Let's go home now, okay?"

"Yeah, home now."

THREE

SAM WOULD ALWAYS TEXT FROM WORK THROUGH-out the day. *How's your day* and *Check out this song* and *What are we feeding the kids for dinner?*

That day, the seventh of December, 2015, I'd been at work but away from my desk in meetings, so I didn't register the absence of texts from him until the end of the day, when I returned to grab my stuff and head out the door.

I called him. Straight to voice mail. Not terribly unusual — I figured his phone was out of juice or he'd left it at home, so I tried his office. Someone picked up, and she said some things to me, things like *Sam didn't show up for work today. We can't seem to reach him. We were wondering how to get hold of you to make sure he's okay.*

Sometimes you just know things. I just knew.

If you've ever had intravenous saline, you know the feeling of some kind of alien substance slithering through your veins. That's how the terrible knowing slithered through me. Cold, snakelike.

My sister was the one to call the cops when I phoned her in a panic.

"There's something wrong. He wouldn't not call work. He wouldn't not let them know he wasn't coming in. He'd never do that."

"Maybe his phone died," she said, "and he's not feeling well enough to charge it."

She offered to go over and check my house herself, but I said no.

"Okay, listen," she said. "I'm sure he's fine, but I'll phone the non-emergency number for a wellness check, and you just come to my place."

She said everything would be fine. So did my co-worker, who drove my van for me to pick up Benji because I couldn't. I was trembling and had to focus on supplying my brain with enough oxygen to not pass out. I tried box breathing: in for four, hold for four, out for four. I tried to slap away the visions of police cars and ambulances with their silent lights flashing in our driveway.

When I arrived at my sister's house, I asked for any news.

"I'm sure he's fine," she said again, "but no news yet. I called again to ask, but they wouldn't tell me anything because I'm not immediate family. They probably haven't checked yet. I bet they'll call any minute to say he answered the door in his underwear."

"Did you ask if the car is in the driveway?"

"I did, but they wouldn't tell me."

"I didn't kiss him goodbye this morning. He slept in the spare room, and I didn't kiss him goodbye. I always kiss him goodbye, and I didn't."

"He's going to be fine, Elsie. He's been weird lately, right?"

He had been weird lately. Distant, impulsive, irritable. And of course there was the booze, his other great love. Was it possible that he'd poured himself into such a violent hangover that he was still passed out?

A knock at the door. My sister leaned over me and put her hands on my shoulders, looked firmly into my eyes.

"We ordered pizza," she said. "It's just the pizza guy."

But it wasn't the pizza guy at all.

O

I have become, in the last ten years, somewhat familiar with grieving. I know the stages well, how they all jumble together like in a bingo cage.

The losses went like this: Mom, Dad, Love of Life.

I don't remember being this angry after my parents died. I was sad, bereft. I felt robbed and forlorn, but it wasn't like this, where I think *Fuck you* at nearly everyone I cross paths with. At the young couple kissing at the crosswalk light: *You have no idea what life will take from you.* At the baby boomer ladies with their sensible haircuts power walking together, their arms bent into stiff right angles and their thin lips flapping. At the little kids at the park, their bright, plump faces flushed from play: *Your parents are flawed and mortal, and so are you in ways you will discover slowly and painfully.* There is a volcano in me, primitive, pre-verbal. It's anger, pressured anger at every atom of matter arrogantly blinking in and out of existence. *Fuck you, matter.*

Rage is a normal part of the grieving process, that's what all the memes say. It's standard best practice to hate everything for a while. It's also a rational response to the justified concern that more will be taken away. The problem is that it's not in my nature to cling to anger this way. With every *Fuck you*, I can feel my heart shrinking. It's probably shrivelled to the size of a plum by now.

At its core, grief is a very self-involved and childish way of being in the world. There must be a reason we regress to this childlike state. It must offer some protection, some comfort, even if it feels like being left alone in a crib for three days with an evil clown stuffy grinning at you from the dresser. I wonder when it will end, the intensity of the bitterness. It's exhausting being mad all the time. I'm exhausted. Will I wake up one day and find it has evaporated in my sleep, that I am suddenly capable of empathy and joy, that I forgive everything and am overwhelmed by compassion and gratitude and goodwill toward my fellow creatures? If so, what can I do to get to that place quicker? I've tried sweating it out at boot camp. I've tried primal screams while driving alone through Mount Douglas Park. Nothing has worked.

I am basically wearing contact lenses made of pond slime. Everything I see is offensive. Everyone I encounter appears smug in their wholeness, their togetherness, their blissful, normal, stupid luckiness at probably not having a loss that defines every moment of their lives. There must be some way to expedite this stage of the process.

I know there isn't. I'm stuck here on Anger Island with my third Tim Hortons double-double of the day, glaring at the mom and dad seated at the picnic table next to me as my toddler spins in circles on the grass instead of exploring the climbing structure. This is the park where Sam met Lark for the first time. She was four years old. I look at the swing set now, remember pushing Lark and smiling back at Sam in the low November sun.

Picnic-table mom is arranging some cut-up oranges and crackers on a plate for her kids. When she's done, she straddles the bench in front of her husband, and he puts an arm around her waist, lifts up her ponytail to kiss her neck. *Fuck these people.* After the park, we hit the grocery store. An old hippie fills his basket with grapefruit and thyme. He smiles and says, "Hey, big guy!" to my son, but I suspect he's really thinking about following me to my car and hiding behind a cedar hedge. He will watch me place my groceries in the trunk and fasten the car-seat buckles before he deploys the old rag-over-the-mouth routine and drags me behind a Dumpster full of rotting cabbage and expired bread. He will pull a jagged grapefruit spoon from the pocket of his Guatemalan vest, scoop out my eyes and eat them, cut out my tongue and throw it into a tree, slice off my breasts, devour them, too.

I spend the entire drive home watching this film play out. My son left alone, screaming *Mama* in his car seat. His mama is in pieces.

The intrusive thoughts of an animal mind on high alert is what's going on here: a chubby little fist of nerves at the top of the spine throwing chemical and electrical punches at ghosts in the dark, hijacking the nervous system, flooding the whole silly organism with adrenalin and cortisol in an endless, endless loop of imaginary threats and fight-or-flight responses. I know this. We have lizard brains buried in there, all of us. But I wonder, is it all that remains when you strip everything else away? *Fuck you, amygdala.*

I have developed some positive coping strategies for when I get real out of sorts from the PTSD. Talking to myself in the second person using a Pema Chödrön voice is one that I'm particularly proud of.

Like so:

You should picture a stop sign.

No, you should picture all your thoughts as fallen leaves. Yes, down they twirl, landing on the surface of a lazy river.

You are detached from these thoughts. You are not your thoughts — you are not even the you that you think you are. You are not the leaves, nor the tree they fell from. You are just the observer of all these silly things, and they are all so silly — so silly that they should make you giggle and coo like a happy infant.

You — the real you — are outside of time, floating through the nothingness inside a safe, loving soap bubble. The soap bubble was blown by the mouth of your mother (a soft and beautiful mouth, not the mouth she had when she was dying of cancer and got that white goo in the corners), and inside the bubble you are lying in the sun under a tree, listening to the distant fingerpicking of an acoustic guitar, eating space berries, and drinking milk from the big, pillowy breasts that hang from the trunk of the tree. Which is a magnolia tree, by the way.

Maybe the real me really *is* an old and wise and calm and stoic observer outside of time and space. Maybe it really wants for nothing and is completely unattached to the perceptions of the dumb, grieving ape to which it is bound. The real me isn't grieving, because it can't feel pain. It doesn't care about material things like nice-smelling shampoo and sheets with decent thread counts and whether that coffee is fair trade.

Benji is napping in his crib. I go to the bathroom, take off my pants, and start dry-shaving my labia with my leg propped on the toilet seat. Then I get up onto the counter to inspect the mess. It's all cut up, but who cares? Unless I end up in a serious accident on my way to work tomorrow and some handsome ER doc has to examine every inch of me, then I might care. Caring would be a nice change.

FOUR

SAM WROTE QUITE UNLIKE ANYONE ELSE I'VE EVER
encountered. His turns of phrase were unusual and poetic, and
his writing was beautiful, though he put his commas in strange
places. He overused them, his commas. He put them in places,
like this, where he would normally pause, in the middle of his
very particular and stilted and excited way of finding a path
through the thick of his ideas.

It was hard not to edit every message he sent me.

Now I go through my emails, read his messages, and imagine each comma, as him, taking, a breath.

In the weeks after our first date, we participated in the
time-honoured mating ritual of sending links to songs on
YouTube and writing about all the ways they made us feel
about life and each other. I sent him "Silly Love" by Daniel
Johnston and talked about how I could never imagine love
being requited before meeting him, and also how Johnston
wouldn't have made the same music with the same sincerity

without the scourge of mental illness, how beautifully sad it all was.

From: Sam <QBit_Sam@vergemail.com>
Date: November 28, 2010 at 3:28 p.m.
Subject: Daniel Johnston
To: Elsie J. <Elsiejane@vergemail.com>

The song you sent by Daniel Johnston about un-requited love. I love it. I do, and yet I wonder if we hear it differently. To me, it radiates gentleness and yearning, both of which I relate to, deeply. You mentioned his sincerity, which is something I never really think about when I'm consuming art. Is that a thing, consuming art? Maybe appreciating is a better word. I guess it's because I'm not an artist, and I'm not attuned to the process of creation and exhibition. I suppose I don't much care where something comes from, or the process it moves through to get there. Sincere or insincere, all that matters to me about art is that it rings true, and makes me feel something.

Speaking of unrequited love, "Downtown Train" is my favourite song that speaks to the obsession and yearning that drive limerence, which is what unrequit-ed love really is. It's not love, not *true* love, but a state of passionate fixation. It can be beautiful. It changes you, biochemically, gets you high. Head in the clouds, acute insomnia, guts swirling, heart crawling with stars. Limerence is a crush on steroids. And like most things that feel so good and so bad simultaneously, it's probably not a very healthy state to be in, long-term.

It's simply not a sustainable state. The fact that it can happen with or without mutuality is also a problem. Some people cross the line, and find themselves alone on the other side, stalking the idea of a person and confusing chemicals with love. You're not a hopeless romantic at that point, you're just another creepy fuck.

You know this song, I'm sure, "Downtown Train." But here's the link, anyway: https://www.youtube.com/watch?v=dQw4w9WgXcQ.

My heart still skips a beat, whenever I hear it. It brings me right back to this one evening in 1994, in early Spring. I was drinking whisky on Willows Beach, waiting for a friend to join me to take in the sunset (and then go to the bars and get up to all kinds of other nonsense), and I saw this girl. She was walking along the shore a few yards behind her group of friends. I recognized her as my crush from philosophy class. I'd tried to muster the courage to speak to her all semester. Every day I'd sort of hang around and watch her put her books in her bag, but whenever she looked at me, I freaked out and lost my nerve. At the time, I thought she was the most beautiful being I'd ever seen. And then there she was, walking right past me on the beach. I thought about calling out to her, saying hello. I almost did. I never saw the girl again, and I often wonder about the Sam in a parallel universe who said hello and introduced himself. Strange, how some seemingly insignificant things stick with us.

I am enjoying our email exchanges. I'm so curious about you. I want more.

-Sam

I lie in the bed we used to share and pore over the hundreds of emails Sam sent to me, looking for hints of what was to come, and when I find none, I pore over them again and find foreshadowing in every word.

I'm sure that losing a spouse sucks for everyone, but when it happens forty years ahead of schedule, it's an extra-big bummer. People just can't relate, and they don't want to. I don't blame them, but in case you're wondering: Initially, it feels like an earthquake, the foundation of your life and future shaken, the landscape permanently altered. Then comes the sense of betrayal, which is likely specific to those of us who lose partners to the catastrophic Judas kiss of addiction. It is very difficult to weasel your way out of feeling magnificently betrayed, and yet the flip side of betrayal is the sense of culpability, which is arguably worse.

O

For our first date, we met outside a coffee shop on Johnson Street. The details were arranged through a phone call that took place after a week of exchanging messages on OkCupid. *I'll call you at 8, after your daughter is in bed*, he wrote, and he did exactly that. From 8:00 p.m. to 8:01 p.m. I stood at the kitchen counter and watched the phone ring until it went to voice mail. I was hoping he'd leave a message, so if he had a creepy voice, I could just never call back and block him on the dating site, but he didn't leave one.

I paced until 8:27 with the phone in my hand, dialling half the number at least a dozen times before I summoned the courage to plunk in the entire thing. I squeezed my face shut and held my breath until he picked up.

"'Lo?"

"It's Elsie."

"I know, you gave me your number."

Where was the *How are you?* Where was the *Thanks for calling me back?*

"Right, of course. So how are you?"

"Fine. Does eight tomorrow work? The Seven Ten coffee shop on Johnson."

"Sure, that sounds great. Yeah, eight works for me. Awesome. How are you?"

"See you then."

"Wait, should I tell you what I'm going to be wearing, or …?"

He had already hung up. This was very unromantic, and I was not impressed.

I still wasn't sure about meeting him. He was bald, and I was only twenty-nine, which felt much too young to kiss a bald man.

"Baldies need love, too," said my workmate when I showed her his profile in the lunchroom. She took my phone to inspect him while she ate her sandwich. "Ooh, yeah, he looks super nerdy; I bet he has a huge penis."

Sam's profile name was Rain_Dogs2. When you get a message on OkCupid, you can see only the first few words. In this case, I was alerted to a new message from Rain_Dogs2 that said *Hi! What is your […],* and I ignored it for a couple of days. I assumed it said something like *What is your digits mmmmmmm-yeah a beutiful sexy ass grl lol love it,* and I'd already decided not to respond to anyone who used *lol* or *sexy* or *girl* in their first message. *Ass* would be fine, but none of the others. Also, I was busy chatting with Nathan, username Fire_U_Up, a firefighter with a head of messy blond curls who regaled me with tales of battling wildfires by hanging from a helicopter. It was going really well until he wrote *Wasn't sure who Kurt Vonnegut was, LOL, had to google that!*, which made it clear we weren't soulmates after all. I opened my other messages.

> *Rain_Dogs2 wrote:*
> Hi! What is your kid's favourite cartoon?

Rain_Dogs2 had the most atrocious profile pic I'd seen yet: a blurry shot taken from a desktop webcam in a dark room. Retro glasses with thick black frames, the glare of the computer screen reflecting off the lenses and totally obscuring his eyes. His face was bathed in the deeply unattractive yellow-blue light beloved of chat-room groomers and online poker addicts hiding from their wives the world over.

I scrolled down to his *About Me.*

As I near mid-life, it read, *I find myself thinking a lot about puzzles.*

The rest of his profile was a surprising delight. Dense and eccentric, threaded all through with curiosity and longing and so many, many, many commas. Three whole paragraphs on artificial intelligence and the singularity; a paragraph about how the song "Lost Coastlines" by Okkervil River seemed written for this moment in his life; a jokey bit about how messy his apartment was; two paragraphs concerning the philosophical conundrum of free will; and then back to the puzzles and how, when we're born, we're given a bag full of puzzle pieces but no image for reference. How we spend our lives trying to fit all the pieces together so we can see the whole picture. We assume the pieces we were given were the right ones in the first place, and then what if they weren't? What then?

I decided to respond. What the hell, right? At the very least, a conversation about cartoons would be a palate cleanser.

E-Jay wrote:
Hey! My daughter is into SpongeBob, but I like Scooby-Doo. What's your favourite?

Rain_Dogs2 wrote:
My son likes Scooby-Doo, too. You're beautiful, by the way. Or your pictures are beautiful, at least, and they must capture something, about you. I bet you tire of hearing that on this website. I bet most women do. But I really mean it. I like your profile, you're a great writer. You are also far too young for me, but I read your words and felt compelled to reach out, to say hello, and to tell you, that I enjoyed reading every word. I liked it, I think I'd like you. You seem weird, and funny. That's a great combo. I think we would like each other, if you don't mind me saying so. As I said, you are too young for me, and I don't expect any more than friendship, from this website. I am just dipping my toe in this world of online dating.

You have great taste in music. Tom Waits is a favourite of mine, too, if you couldn't tell from my username.

I wrote back saying that my photos were deceptive and I actually had a tumour on the back of my neck with hair and teeth and a thumb. I was annoyed by the "friendship" comment. Nobody goes on a dating website looking for friendship.

We went back and forth furiously for a few days, and with each message I tiptoed over the line between making everything a stupid joke and earnestly oversharing. He was so sincere, so genuine and playful and interesting, that I found myself responding at times in a way I wasn't accustomed to: honestly, thoroughly. Probably too thoroughly for a dating website, I decided.

E-Jay wrote:
It feels weird having messages popping up from dudes asking if I'm horny while I'm in the middle of writing to you about my father's meningitis and sub- sequent brain injury and subsequent suicide attempt and hospitalization for catatonic depression. Can we move this conversation somewhere more private? My email address is elsiejane@vergemail.com.

Rain_Dogs2 wrote:
What a superb idea. I will email you, Elsie Jane (is Jane your middle name?) to ask if you are horny, but in a subtler way. Expect it.

O

When I arrived at the coffee shop to meet Sam that night, it was closed. There was nobody in sight. No street lamps, either. It was drizzling rain and I was waiting in the dark, fidgeting against a garbage can and regretting the thong that was burrowing rudely into the folds of my labia.

He was late. Three minutes. Eight minutes. Nine minutes.

I was about to give up when I saw a silhouette sauntering toward me from down the block. Someone in a trench coat.

Oh no, he's a trench coat person. But no, it wasn't a trench coat. It was a leather jacket that was far, far too large for this man's body. It hung almost to his knees.

I stiffened, braced myself for a terrible, awkward evening, and walked cautiously toward him.

"Hello, Rain Dogs Two?"

"Hi, Elsie Jane."

He went in for a hug, but I did one of those slick *No way, sir* moves that all women have mastered and stuck out my hand for a shake. He chuckled.

"Place is closed, huh? Guess I should have checked the hours."

"Yeah. It's pretty dark here. I hope you don't murder me."

We decided on another coffee place a block away. Walking under street lamps, I got a good look at his face for the first time, saw his eyes.

We ended up at Smith's Pub that night. We drank beer, talked about movies and books and all the places we wanted to see in the world. In the spaces between words, we stared at each other with stupid grins and shy blinks. Butterflies. Fireworks. The sense of cosmic knowing.

"You look so familiar," he said as we waited for a cab and shared a cigarette.

"Yeah. Yeah, you too."

"Maybe we've been in line together at the grocery store? Do you shop at Hudson's?"

"I do! That must be it."

"We've definitely seen each other before."

"Definitely."

"I mean, we did look at pictures of each other on the internet."

"Right, yeah. Except with the way your glasses reflected the computer screen, I couldn't really see your eyes. It's your eyes that are familiar. So weird."

"Yours, too. Your eyes. I wonder where else we've been right next to each other before?"

O

In that place outside of time and space, that's where. I felt it then; I know it now.

Unfortunately, knowing about the place outside of time and space does not mean I get to skip work in the morning. I have to be up in less than three hours, and since I haven't slept yet, I may as well give up. I pace the house. I smoke a cigarette on the patio, watch a wood bug crawl over my naked big toe, pick it up and flick it over the fence into Starla's yard and think about how great it would be if I could just throw all my garbage and recycling over there.

Back inside, I pick up my guitar. I've been playing and writing songs since I was twelve, but I've had to be judicious about it since Benji was born. He's sensitive to certain noises and guitar happens to be chief among them, so I have to be stealthy about it, to sneak around and sing and play only when he's sleeping, which is what I'm doing now as I finish up a song I'm calling "Death Star Cookie Jar."

It goes like this:

An elegant place for your loved one's remains
We'll help you figure it out
We have black ones and red ones
For all of your dead ones

Buy two and get a discount
Death Star cookie jar
The perfect place for you to sleep
To go inside and have some dreams

Death Star cookie jar! Death Star cookie jar!
[x 3, then fade to complete and total
  nothingness]

O

From: Sam <QBit_Sam@vergemail.com>

Date: December 4, 2010 at 4:46 a.m.

Subject: Re: Cohen

To: Elsie J. <Elsiejane@vergemail.com>

That kiss, tonight, after the concert. I'm sorry if I
came on too strong. You seemed taken aback, and
then I felt awkward. I worry that I am moving too
fast for you. Please tell me, if that's the case, so I can
calibrate.

I'd like to penetrate your bubble, because I see
that beyond it is someone I like very much, if I could
only move through it. It will take time, to get to know
each other's rhythms, recognize each other's quirks.
I just hope I didn't scare you off. I can see, in hindsight, that kissing you so enthusiastically while we
were standing in a windstorm outside a Wendy's restaurant, especially right after realizing my car had
been towed, was a bit weird. Elsie, I'm a bit weird.
Sometimes I feel like I don't really live in this world, or
understand the rules. But I hope you'll let me get to

know you better, and let me through your bubble. I'll just have to be more patient, and less weird. I'm fine with that, if you'll have me.

You said tonight that you don't want expectation, but I can't help it, I expect things. I expect to keep falling in love with you, forever. I know how it sounds. It's cheesy shit, but it's true, and I want you to know that cheesy shit and commitment don't scare me. Not in relationships, not anywhere else in life. Maybe that's where we're different, in how vulnerable we're willing to be. I'll crack jokes and throw myself in the deep end without a temperature check first, for better or for worse, and risk drowning. I'll jump out of a plane when I have absolutely no reason to believe I'm even wearing a parachute. And you know what? I'm covered in bruises from it.

Some people are born with more heart than sense. Elsie, I'm one of them.

-Sam

FIVE

I'M A CONCERNS OFFICER WORKING WITHIN WHAT I like to call the Ministry of Heartache. My job is to receive care complaints from patients and families after they have shitty experiences in the health care system. Sometimes the concerns are legitimately horrifying (a surgeon amputated the wrong hand), sometimes they're petty (a nurse gave someone's grandma the stink eye). I got this job when I finished my master's in organizational psychology, and after ten years of working on the front lines in community mental health, a desk job felt like a reprieve from tragedy and chaos. It didn't take me long to figure out that I was merely peering out a different window at the same pain.

In this job, everyone hates me. Patients and families hate me because I represent a health care system that wronged them. Health Authority staff hate me because I'm annoying them and making them feel bad about themselves by sharing complaints and demanding a response when they're all working hard to serve patients. Also, I operate under legislated deadlines that are sometimes impossible to meet. Since I returned to work the month after Sam died, I can't focus for more than five minutes on anything that requires me to move logically from one activity to another.

All of this means that I must spend a great deal of time hiding in the bathroom (or by the delivery trucks behind my office building, smoking with the parking lot security guards). My colleagues don't seem to notice my frequent absences, or maybe they're turning a blind eye because they feel sorry for me. I'm fine with that. Everyone around here now regards me with pity and fear. Except Rod, here. I've just snuck out for my second smoke break of the morning, and there's a security guard I've never seen before. I know his name is Rod because of his name tag, and I can't help but also note his striking resemblance to Rodney Dangerfield, which is both stirring and upsetting. What are the chances?

I know I shouldn't point out the Dangerfield likeness, but since Sam died, I've lost what little filter I had.

"Hey, did you know that Rodney Dangerfield's tombstone says *There goes the neighborhood*?"

"Sorry?"

"Did you know that Rodney Dangerfield's tombstone says *There goes the neighborhood*? Ha!"

"Right."

"You remind me of Rodney Dangerfield. Has anyone ever told you that?"

His face hardens. He thinks I'm making fun of him. I'm not. I'm sincerely trying to form a friendly bond with Rod, to affirm our shared humanity while we smoke, but it's too late to explain that now. He thinks I'm a fuckface.

"It's just that your name tag says *Rod*, so I thought it was funny."

"Do you know how many times a day I hear the Rodney Dangerfield thing?"

"I'm sorry."

He flicks his smoke away and takes his leave, still shaking his head in disgust as he climbs the parkade stairs. The cigarette lands below a lilac bush, burns off. A pair of wild bunnies hop out, and they sniff at it, hoping it's a crumb of food. My celebrity anecdotes don't usually land this badly.

If I had a better personality, I could probably achieve great things. I could create a charitable foundation to help other young families shattered by grief. I could do TEDx Talks about how grief is actually a gift and an opportunity to practise gratitude for the things you still have in your life. At the very least, I could be an excellent mother who sets a good example by getting up at 5:00 a.m. and meditating and then eating dewy ferns during my forest run and then preparing a delicious vegan breakfast hash with freshly squeezed pomegranate juice. I can't even do that. I spend the very little free daylight time I have compulsively jamming my brain with pointless garbage on the internet. Reddit, *The Onion*, celebrity gossip sites, CNN. Even here at the office, I can't help but check. I am currently sitting on the toilet reading Lainey Gossip to calm myself down after the cigarette-sniffing bunnies made me cry. I felt jealous of them, of their kinship in bunnydom. I imagined Sam and me, reincarnated as bunnies, hopping all around and sniffing things together, nibbling clovers and twigs and conifers. The bliss that would be. *Fuck you, bunnies.*

I pull myself together and make it to the photocopier. This is a task I can manage because there is only one button involved, and even though I'm using hospital equipment for personal reasons (copying Sam's death certificate, if you must know), I feel a sense of pride and accomplishment pushing this button.

The Risk Management Coordinator emerges from the lunchroom and startles when she sees me, clearly uncomfortable about being in such close proximity to the Cursed One. She gives me a wincing smile and long blink, but she doesn't dare speak to me. She scurries away, afraid perhaps that my grieving-person smell might infect her life.

Smell it. Know it.

Back at my desk, there is a new file on my keyboard: a complaint from a mother in Abbotsford. Something about how her son was accidentally given a double dose of hydromorphone when he visited the ER with appendicitis. Something about how he had a cardiac arrest and was brought back with Narcan. Then something-something *taken off life support*, something-something *your incompetence murdered my son*.

It's part of my job to call people, acknowledge their complaints, explain the investigation process. The idea of calling this grieving mother fills me with icicles of dread. Still, I pick up the phone and let it ring until a lady picks up.

"Hello."

"Hello, is Maureen available, please?"

"I'm Maureen."

"Good morning, Maureen, thanks for taking my call. This is Elsie from the Ministry of Health care complaints department. How are you this morning?"

"How do you think I am?"

"..."

"Hello?"

"Hi, Maureen."

"Well?"

"Well, I'm just calling to say, firstly, that I'm so very sorry for your loss, and I can't imagine what you must be experiencing right now."

"No. You certainly can't."

"I know. I can't, and I want to acknowledge that, and to say thank you for bringing this to our attention. If it's okay, I'd like to share with you a bit about what to expect from the complaints process?"

"How old are you? You sound young."

"I'm thirty-four."

"Well, isn't that nice for you. My son was twenty-four. *Twenty. Four.*"

"I see that, Maureen, from your email. I know it's not easy."

"You *know*, do you? How do you *know*? Do you have children?"

"I do, I ha—"

"Lady, don't you dare tell me you *know.*"

"I'm sorry, Maureen."

"Stop calling me Maureen! Don't say my name. You have *no idea*. You, lady, are a robotic bureaucrat. Do you know whose life you've stolen?"

"Evan. Evan's life."

"Don't say his name. My son was an athlete — how about that? He spent his summers volunteering at a camp for *poor* kids!"

"He sounds like a wonderful man."

"He was still a child!"

"He was still so youn—"

"He was on the *national rowing team* —"

My hand slams the phone onto the receiver.

I have just hung up on grieving Maureen. I didn't mean to; it was my hand that did it. My hand, recognizing a voice too familiar in its pain and rage. All that feeling crashing through the phone lines might cause them to snap and light everything on fire, so it's probably safer for everyone that my hand hung up.

Time to hide in the bathroom again before someone notices my chin quivering.

I turn on the hand dryer so nobody will hear me hyperventilating and pouring my sad snakes all over the floor. When this batch is mostly out of me, I sit on the toilet and scroll through *The Onion* until there's a knock on the door.

"Just a sec! Almost done!"

You know, you could be coping better by now if you'd just try a little bit harder, my mother clucks at me as I lean over the sink and try to splash the swollen redness off my face.

Shhhhh, I tell her. I look at the poster on the door: a doctor, grinning in his scrubs with soapy suds in his hands. *Handwashing!* it shouts. *Choose YES today!*

Another knock on the door.

"Just a *second!* Sorry, I just have to do one more thing!"

I stand up straight, put my hands in the air for a dead-eyed power pose and whisper:

"Today ...

"I choose ...

"No!"

You can petition the universe for abundance, but if you're shattered and angry, the universe will see right through you. Why bother trying?

I unlock the door for the poor pregnant admin assistant waiting to pee. She looks terrified and slinks past me.

Smell it. Know it.

If grief had a smell, it would be hot dog juice. The hot dog juice smell has sunk into my skin and become part of my identity, and letting go of it means letting go of love. I pine for Sam and the life that was supposed to be. It's not just what I do, it's become who I am.

And what of it, anyway? What kind of a person lets go of love?

From: Sam <QBit_Sam@vergemail.com>

Date: December 15, 2010 at 10:42 p.m.

Subject: colours

To: Elsie J. <Elsiejane@vergemail.com>

I know that asking you to be with me is a huge bet. I know it is, that it's a big bet for you. And yes, I'm writing to you again, but it's only because waiting for your response is making me feel insane. I can't do anything else, right now, but think of you. Really, I can't. I know I'm asking you to bet on me, and I know you don't have to do it. I only want you to make a bet you believe in, but I'm going to keep upping the ante until you show your hand. That's probably not a fair thing to do, especially since you'll eventually see that I've got nothing. That I've been playing with rags.

It's not victory I'm looking for, in this. It's intimacy. I want to be as near to you as possible, as close as possible, but only if you want that, too. Do you, darling? I can go there, to that level of intimacy, but only if you want to. Only if you go there, too.

I want more, with you, than I've ever wanted with anybody. I want to eat the world with you, and I know it's possible. Because of how you write, and speak, and how tender you can be. We can eat the world, together, Elsie. We can go all the way. It's all I want, in this life.

You talked about your mother last night, how you went down to the bottom of the lake in your grief. I've been there, too, to the bottom of things, but for different reasons. What I found down there was a true, animal hunger for intimacy.

Elsie, you have such a tender heart. I can see it, in how you move in the world, which is a cruel place. It's cruel because people are confused. They don't know what they want, and they seek fulfillment in ways that bring pain.

I have never been more sure of anything in my life than wanting you. To be close to you, and eat the world with you. Sure, I want intimacy, but it can't be with just anyone. It has to be with you.

This isn't a gasp for air, with me. More, it's a gasp for life. I've never met anyone else like you. I can't believe I found you. I can't believe I did.

-Sam

SIX

TONIGHT IS GOING TO BE MY FIRST NIGHT WITHOUT kids since Sam died. I'm going to wear pretty clothes, drink wine, have romantic conversations. Hopefully I'm going to be seduced by Saul. Who's Saul? He's my friend, or he was before Sam died. He's a different kind of friend now, a friend who may or may not be a friend at all.

I met him back in 2011. Sam and I were at a pub for a Tom Waits tribute night. We went to shows every weekend before Benji was born. I was also part of that particular show (covering "Dirt in the Ground" and "Earth Died Screaming"). After my set, Saul approached us on the pub patio with a business card. *Saul Waters*, it read, *Literary Shit Disturber*. He was a writer, he told us, and new in town. He'd just come from Calgary and was starting up an arts and culture website that he was looking to promote.

I watched him make the rounds with his business cards. He was friendly, boisterous, a little bit goofy, roguishly handsome in the manner of a young Jeff Bridges. At last call, he climbed drunkenly onto the pub counter and shouted along in a ridiculous baritone to "Christmas Card from a Hooker in Minneapolis." I was intrigued, because who wouldn't be intrigued by a person willing to make such a spectacle of themselves?

Sam did not share my enthusiasm.

"I just got a Facebook friend request from that guy at the Tom Waits night," he said the next morning.

"Oh? The funny one who sang on the counter?"

"It wasn't that funny."

I'd received a request, too, had accepted immediately, and was even more intrigued when I saw his posts about writing a novel.

I said, "He friend-requested me, too, and I looked at his website. He's writing a novel, apparently."

"So what? Who isn't?"

"I mean, not everyone is. Some people aren't writing a novel."

"Do you wish I was a writer?"

"No, I'm happy that you design software, and I think machine learning is art. You're an artist."

"Do you think he's handsome?"

"Who?"

"Don't do that. You know who."

"Yeah, fine, he's handsome. And he's a total fucking weirdo, so I want to be Facebook friends with him."

That's all we were, really, Facebook friends, so I was surprised when he showed up to Sam's funeral. While I was in the receiving line, I noticed him standing in the corner of the lobby wearing a peacoat and a huge wool scarf, unshaven, his hair wild with messy curls. It was startling to see him there. He looked ragged and out of place. I waved. He raised his glass of lemon water at me. When I looked for him at the reception, he was gone, but in those first weeks after Sam died, he was there for me. He was unafraid to text me, which is more than I can say for many of my closer friends. He sent me links to Rilke poems to help me feel better about loving a dead person. He emailed me a draft of his novel so I could focus on Great Canadian Literature instead of grief.

My sister was suspicious of his sudden interest.

"I don't like it. He's like a vulture circling a dead cow."

"Are you calling me a cow?"

"I'm saying this feels gross. You're vulnerable. He better not try getting romantic with you, or I'll slit his throat."

But I was grateful for the attention, the distraction. He was the only person who would come over just to hang out with me. Sure, it was mostly because the heat and electricity had been cut off in his apartment and he needed warmth and light, but hey, he was *there*. He let me go on and on about Sam and my parents until the wee hours of the morning. And he was more serious one to one than when we had bumped into him at shows. He was actually a very quiet, lovely person, I decided, who masked his shyness with a rowdy and ridiculous persona modelled after his literary heroes (Ginsberg and Kerouac, obviously).

After a couple of weeks of him texting me from whatever pub he was at downtown and then walking all the way to the suburbs to sleep on my couch, we had sex. At the time, I thought it was the best sex I'd ever had. I was so lonely and starved for reassurance that I was still a vital being that I could have been seduced by an alien insect and it would have been just as thrilling. It's not something I would have expected, if someone had told me the love of my life would die, this urgency to feel loved, desired.

"I remember the first time I saw you," Saul said during one of our midnight cigarettes on my back porch. "I was mesmerized."

We went back into the living room, and he sat very close to me on the couch.

"Can I hold your hand?" he asked.

"Sure."

The touch of his hand against mine was electric, and before I knew it, we were on the carpet, tearing off each other's clothes, inhaling each other's faces. Then we were up against the wall, and he was inside me, his hands in my hair. When he came, he made a sound like Scooby-Doo does when he laughs. It was all very romantic, except for the part when Benji woke up on account of the Scooby-Doo noises and my milk came flooding through my T-shirt at the sound of my baby's cry.

"Whoa," said Saul, staring at my chest like it was an exploding building. "Dude, that's *crazy*."

I made him hide in the kitchen while I brought Benji upstairs and nursed him on the couch. Saul turned on the faucet, presumably getting himself a glass of water. Benji unlatched from my nipple and swivelled his head around excitedly.

"Dada?"

He climbed off me and toddled into the kitchen, where he discovered Saul leaning against the cupboards on the floor and drinking from one of his sippy cups.

"Awww," Saul said. "Hey, little fella."

Benji climbed up me like a little chimp and hid his face in the crook of my neck.

"Sorry," I told Saul, "I've got to get him back to sleep. Do you mind sleeping on the couch?"

"I don't mind at all. You look beautiful right now, by the way."

"Oh, thanks."

Exposing your child to this strange man in the middle of the night, tsk-tsked my mother. *I'm appalled.*

O

Somehow Saul wasn't appalled, and he wasn't scared away. He showed up at my door, night after night, with windswept curls drenched in winter rain. The smell of him, the stale beer and man-sweat smell, comforted and aroused me. There were weeks of hot and heavy sex on the floor, against the walls, in the kitchen, in the bed. A veritable frenzy of manic humping, every orgasm a middle finger in the air to Sam, to the slaughtered promise of the life that was supposed to be, to the indifference of a universe that gives so generously and then snatches it all away.

Unfortunately, and seemingly out of nowhere, a few weeks ago Saul decided that my vagina and my grieving-person stories weren't to his liking after all. He stopped showing up. He ghosted me. This was a very confusing turn of events. I simply could not accept that I'd been selected for sampling and then tossed aside, so I did what any human in this situation would do: Though he wasn't speaking to me anymore, I sent him an email demanding that he never, ever speak to me again.

I am removing myself from your world, I wrote, *for my own well-being.*

He responded with a brief and businesslike *I understand*, so I did the most dignified thing and followed up with a series of increasingly unhinged emails sent between midnight and 4:00 a.m., some pleading for him to please be in love with me but also leave me alone, some soliciting an objective list of what exactly was wrong with me, some imploring him to forgive me my hysterical woman-brain, a couple others to advise him that he was the worst person in the entire world for pursuing me so intensely at my most vulnerable and then compounding my feelings of abandonment by discarding me. In the last one, I wished him a happy birthday and told him I had a gift for him (I do — a leather-bound journal I'd bought before he ghosted), then begged him to meet me at Clive's Classic Lounge, as friends, just friends.

O

"I hate that guy," my sister said.

We were feeding ducks with the kids at Beacon Hill Park.

"I knew this would happen. I knew he was pursuing you and fucking with you. He started texting you when Sam's body was still warm, and I *told* you this was what he was doing. What a fucking asshole."

"No, it's me. There's something wrong with me."

"There is nothing wrong with you. You wouldn't give him the time of day if you weren't grieving like this. God, I hate him."

"*Benji, too close to the pond, sweetie!* Then why did he drop me like I'm garbage?"

"Because he's a Lothario piece of shit."

No, I told her, he wasn't a piece of shit. He was the only person who had helped me feel visible and vital and like I could be whole again one day. It was me who had fucked it up. I'd talked too much about my grief, about my dead parents, about my dead love.

○

I arrived home from the park and found a response from Saul in my email. Against what was most certainly his better judgment, he agreed to meet me at Clive's Classic Lounge. I called my sister immediately, asked if she could take my kids overnight.

"What's this for?"

"A self-care date. With myself."

"You're sure you're not meeting Saul? Because I'm not doing this if you're going to meet that creep."

"I'm sure. He doesn't like me anymore. It's just a self-care night."

○

Sometimes self-care means lying to your sister in case a man who rejected you has changed his mind and decided that he's actually deeply in love with you and needs to ravish you from head to toe until it's Scooby-Doo time.

I feel certain Saul will seduce me again if he sees me all dolled up instead of looking like the slob I was last time he came over, when he commented on my period-stained sweatpants. I'm determined to look normal and attractive tonight.

I shave my armpits, spray some perfume on my labia and butthole, put on fishnet tights and a spaghetti-strap tank top. I pile my hair in a bun and try to follow a YouTube video where a teenage girl from Alabama gives me a tutorial on how to do a classic smoky eye. "Girl," she says, "I got your back."

You're a saucy little slut, says my reflection, and my mother agrees, but then she says, *This is* not *how respectable women grieve.*

I ignore them both and do a power pose.

SEVEN

SAUL IS ALREADY SITTING AT A TABLE WHEN I ARRIVE.
He looks bored, pained.

In fact, he spends the entire night with a look on his face
that says *How do I politely get away from this woman?*, which
means I have to drink more to help pretend I don't notice. The
only time he demonstrates any enthusiasm is when he tells me
he's moving to Colombia to teach English and write his next
masterpiece.

I down eight fancy cocktails and four beers, and when I
spill out of Clive's Classic Lounge, the very last thing I need to
do is smoke a thing called marijuana.

We are walking up Burdett Avenue when I announce that
I would like to have some pot. "You have some, right? I think
I'd like to have a doobie now."

"I thought you didn't like pot?"

"I don't. I hate it because it makes me paranoid and
terrified."

"So it's probably not a good idea, then, right?"

"But I actually don't hate it anymore. I actually just love it now."

He looks at me skeptically.

"No, really, I actually do!"

"… Okay."

He lights up the doobie.

I take a puff. Stumble along some more. Get a fuzzy feeling that makes me giggly and full of love.

This is fun, I think, *and now I should try to hold his hand!*

He pulls his hand away.

"Don't touch my hand. Why are you trying to grab my hand?"

"I don't know. I —"

"Don't touch me."

"Okay, but I need some more of that boodie."

"Doobie?"

"Yeah!"

I grab for it.

"Hey, I think you've had enough," he says.

"Oh, do fuck off," I say. Maybe in a British accent. Probably.

I wrestle the thing out of his fingers with mine.

"I'm a doobie lovah now," I exclaim to the night.

I take another toke.

I am in the middle of an impassioned monologue about how I don't care if he doesn't want to hold my hand because I am going to become the greatest slut of them all and sleep with a thousand of the world's most eligible bachelors and joyously contract chlamydia and embrace a life of free-love debauchery and wanton lust, when I start to feel a little bit weird.

It must mean I need another toke. I'm not practised with marijuana, but I remember people in high school talking about getting *baked*, which sounds pretty good right now. I grab the doobie again, suck it like I've just come up from the bottom of a lake.

Three minutes later, I am positively fucked.

O

Anyone who's had a baby will tell you that it takes time to get used to the new shape of things. The deflation, the balloon-empty swollenness of a body after birth. Everything feels split apart and bruised and suffused with mammalian softness.

Sam was so gentle about it.

"Don't touch my stomach," I said. "Please. I mean it."

"I wish you wouldn't move my hand away. I love you. I love your belly."

"I don't. It's a bowl full of jelly now."

"Sit up — turn around. Look at me. This? This is perfect. This is the belly that carried our son. I love every possible version of you."

"Well, I'm sorry that you have to love this version."

"Believe it."

"What if I grew hemorrhoids all over my face and smelled like old bum sweat and burned rubber all the time?"

"I'd probably need to wear a gas mask and lobster gloves, but I'd love that version, too."

"I might as well do that, then, if you're just going to love me anyway."

Even in those twilight-zone weeks after giving birth, when we were both bleary-eyed and exhausted, when my boobs were leaking so much the sheets were soaked in breast milk, we would reach for each other. So, it was the physical aspect of loss, the experience of severed attachment, that was most bewildering after his death. It was a felt sense that was so overwhelming it was impossible to describe, and the best way I can think to describe it now doesn't at all suffice, but here it is: I was without. Before, I was within love, and after, without.

Once, when having sex with Saul, I covered my belly with my hands to hide the softness and stretch marks.

"What are you doing?"

"Just … nothing. Please don't look at my belly."

He stopped and shook his head, looked down at me with cold annoyance.

"Do I not look like I'm turned on right now? *Fuck.*"

O

Shortly after the last sloppy suck of Purple Kush, I find myself slumped against the brick facade of a closed Subway sandwich shop on Blanshard Street.

Saul is kneeling beside me. "What are you doing? Hey, hey hey hey, you okay?"

"I feel weird. I feel so weird. I can't move."

"You drank too much and then you smoked pot. You need to go home and go to bed."

"I think I've been poisoned. Somebody put something in my drink. This can't just be the pot — I can't move."

"Fuck," he says, mostly to himself. "Poisoned? Are you going to tell people I *poisoned* you now? Please don't say that."

"No, I'm not saying you poisoned me, I'm saying this doesn't feel normal. I can't move."

"Listen, I shouldn't have let you have any weed. I'm sorry about that, okay? But you can't tell people that you've been poisoned. People are going to think you're saying *I* poisoned you."

"But it feels like a poison."

"You just need water and to go to bed. I'm going to get you some water."

My pulse feels sluggish, moving through me in deep, resonant thrums, my heart thumping hard.

I try moving my legs, but they're filled with lead.

Though my right hand is resting on my knee, I notice the left one moving up and down, slapping the pavement. It seems to take an hour before I am able to gain control of it, but it happens with a lot of concentration. The left hand is mine again, though barely.

It starts to dawn on me that Saul has gone somewhere.

"Where did he go?" I ask the night, but it sounds more like "Wallhere'dee gah?"

I can hear my voice, but the audio has been decelerated and deepened like they do to voices on *The Fifth Estate* when you see only the silhouette of the person talking. Thick and slow as molasses.

I consider what it might be like to die right here, in front of the same Subway where I purchased tuna sandwiches on Toonie Tuesdays in my early twenties.

If I die here, at least I will die leaning against a place that brought me the happiness of tuna with extra pickles at an affordable price for students on a budget.

How sad it is, I think, that I won't get the chance to say goodbye to my kids.

"Baaahkihlldsssss," I say to the night, waving bye-bye.

I picture someone finding my body in the morning. Kicking at the lump of me. Clearly Saul has jumped ship and I am on my own, facing certain death on the cold concrete. So much for dying with dignity in a nice, warm bed surrounded by candles and crying people, with Joni Mitchell singing "Blue" softly in the background, like my mother did.

Slowly, slowly, I manage to pull my phone from my purse.

I configure my finger in such a way that I can poke it against some numbers.

"Nine-one-one emergency. Do you need police, fire, or paramedics?"

"Haaaahp me."

"Do you need police, fire, or paramedics?"

"Haaaahp. Meeeee."

"You need help? Are you injured, sir?"

"Hahssssssspitah-ool."

"Sir, I can't understand you. Do you need an ambulance? Where are you right now, sir?"

"Haaaaahp. Meeee."

The phone falls. I hear it thud on the ground. I can't reach it. As I fall over in an effort to put my face on the pavement, closer to the receiver, I notice a swirling hole in the centre of my vision, floating toward me from across the boulevard.

It is hovering over the yellow line in the middle of the street.

Death. Coming to get me. Coming to pick me up and take me to heaven where I can eat tuna sandwiches with Sam and Mom and Dad forever.

I close my eyes. Clench them, ready to be sucked into the abyss.

O

Did you know that Bette Davis lost her spouse when she was thirty-five? His name was Arthur. Guy was just walking down the street when he dropped dead. After his death, she became a violent alcoholic.

Pierce Brosnan, on the other hand, was a much more stable individual. Even though he lost his wife when he was thirty-eight, he became James Bond.

I read in a tabloid once about how when Bette drank, she became some kind of bad witch. I can't remember it exactly, but it was something about how she would close all the curtains and pace around her mansion, cackling, throwing china at the walls, muttering spells. She also carried scissors with her everywhere just in case she bumped into one of her nemeses. If she did, she would sneakily snip off bits of their clothing. When she got a good collection of enemy fabric, she'd pile it in a garbage can lid and light it on fire on her veranda, and she would yell incantations and cry and get naked and dance around. I'm not sure if any of that is true, but who cares.

Pierce remarried. He openly admired and squeezed his beautiful new wife's enormous bum in candid beachfront paparazzi shots that were splashed all over the tabloids.

The point is that some people are Bettes and some are Pierces. Bette went nuts; Pierce went 007 and admired big bums before they were cool. Whether I'll be a Bette or a Pierce remains to be seen, but I seem to be leaning in one direction a bit more than the other.

O

I come to inside the ambulance, puking into an elegant cardboard tray.

A young paramedic with a buzz cut is sitting on the fold-down seat across from me, sneering in disgust. I peek out of one eye, searching his face for some kindness. Don't find any. Heave again, then wipe the vomit and drool from my chin.

"Jesus," he says. "What did you take, eh? What did you use tonight, eh, girl?"

More puking.

"She drank a lot, then she smoked some pot. It wasn't very much. But she hasn't taken anything else. I've been with her all night."

Saul. He's in the ambulance.

"She doesn't use drugs. She's not a drug user at all."

"You mean except for the alcohol and marijuana, because those aren't drugs, eh?"

Shame floods me.

Upon arriving at the hospital, I am helped into a wheelchair and pushed into a curtained ER room, where I am vaguely aware of receiving a bolus of IV fluids. I have put a blanket over my head on account of the sharp white ER light, and also to be in disguise just in case the swirling death-hole comes looking for me.

I don't know how long I am under the blanket. I may have fallen asleep, but I'm pulled into awareness by a soft voice calling my name and asking me to please show my face. I peek out and see a doctor, one with dark hair and kind, crinkly eyes.

"You were very dehydrated," she says. "Go home to bed and rest."

"I'm so embarrassed," I say.

She shrugs and puts her index finger to her temple. *Use your head.*

I nod.

Saul, it turns out, is still there with me. I call a cab. He sits in the front and directs the driver to my house. I curl up in the back seat and focus on trying not to breathe annoyingly.

When we get to my place, he comes inside and stands awkwardly while I roll down my pantyhose with great difficulty.

I lumber over to my bed, crawl in, pull the comforter over my head.

"I'm going to walk home now," he says.

"I'm sorry," I say from under the covers. "I'm so very, very sorry. I am so ashamed of myself."

"It's fine. No big deal. I'm going home to bed."

"But … could you stay with me? Please?"

He sighs a huge, heaving sigh. "I'll sleep on the couch."

"Okay. Thank you."

O

When I wake up, the midmorning light is a ball-peen hammer.

There are streaks of vomit all over my dress. My head is pounding.

I hope he's not still here, I think. And then, *I hope he is …*

I peer around the corner to the living room. Saul is sitting on the couch, flipping through a cookbook. Young Jeff Bridges, the sun shining on his curls. I feel a stab of guilt for admiring him, especially since my mother is also whispering, *You have no loyalty, you absolute slut.*

"Hey," I say. "This is my sheepish way of saying 'hey' and being normal after I totally humiliated myself."

"Morning."

"Thanks for staying with me. And thanks for making sure I got home safe. I'm mortified. I'm sorry."

"Hey, we've all been there. No big deal. It's a much bigger deal in your head than it is in reality, I promise. And I really wanted to make sure you weren't going to tell anyone I poisoned you. Ha."

"Should I give you a ride home?"

"That'd be great."

At his house, I get out and give him a hug. He winces.

"I am truly sorry," I say for the two-hundredth time since waking up at the hospital. "I'm so mortified. That was one of the worst experiences of my life."

"No problem," he lies. "It was really nice seeing you."

O

From: Sam <QBit_Sam@vergemail.com>

Date: December 15, 2010 at 8:19 p.m.

Subject: Lost in this dimension

To: Elsie J. <Elsiejane@vergemail.com>

I've told you this before, in a lot of different ways, but sometimes I feel lost in this dimension. I feel like an imposter to the Earth, like everything has sharp edges. You soften things for me. I hope I do the same, and that the world feels like a softer place, now that you know we're in it together. We're so similar, in all the important ways, and so different, too. We complement each other. I can't wait to grow, with you.

I'm all in. I mean it. Believe it, darling. We've been looking for each other for a long, long time.

We are more than just words, written on grains of sand. We were born in these ridiculous mammal bodies, sure, but we're here to do more.

So, let's do it, together. This is more than limerence, you know it is. Let's jump, together, into this river of time and see where it takes us. Let's swim right into the rapids and go together, terrified, but somehow, without a care in the world.

-Sam

EIGHT

I SLEEP ON SAM'S SIDE OF THE BED NOW. WE USED to lie with our spines pressed against each other. There are times, I think he's in bed with me, moments where I reach for him or try to hook my leg around his. Just now, for instance. He's still not here. It's 2:43 a.m. and my bid for sleep has just been ruined by yet another jolt of aloneness.

I get up and wander the house. I put on my headphones, blast the song "Calgary" by Bon Iver at full volume thirteen times, and smoke at least as many cigarettes. I want to smoke more, but the pack is empty, so I rummage through the kitchen drawers, looking for a stale orphan. I don't find one, but I do find the box of contact juggling balls Sam bought two summers ago, when he became obsessed with a YouTube channel called Kinetic Circus and spent hours every evening following along with a series called *Paul's Balls Tutorials*. He was like a kid with stuff like that. I search "contact juggling" in my email and find a message he sent when we first started dating.

From: Sam <QBit_Sam@vergemail.com>
Date: January 23, 2011 at 5:33 p.m.
Subject: Re: Enchantment jugglers
To: Elsie J. <Elsiejane@vergemail.com>

I sent you a contact juggling clip earlier, did you
watch it yet? I've watched it at least a hundred
times. It enchants me. I love the serene, gentle wonder on his face as he guides the ball from arm to
arm. If only I could put my finger on the meaning
this has, for me, and what it touches. It feels sacred.
It's like a religious experience, watching this dude.
Peaceful. And peace sometimes is a stranger, to me.
Less now, since we've found each other. I can't wait
to see you tonight.

-Sam

The religious experience he talked about in that email,
his excitement about every concept or activity that seized his
interest, it was contagious. He planned elaborate weekend-long
dates for us — skiing, ziplining, bungee jumping. We took
boat trips around the harbour meant only for tourists, ferry
rides across the Sound for no reason at all but to breathe in the
sea spray and marvel at the silver waves. And Sam approached
fatherhood with the same delight and curiosity and wonder. All
the things I wasn't allowed to do as a kid, I got to jump into
with Sam. Camping? Fuck yes. We can roast that entire bag of
marshmallows first so we have no room for dinner and then go
swimming in the lake at midnight with sparklers! Oh, the fair
is in town? Fuck yes! We'll be first through the gates and spend
all day wasting every dollar at the midway, taking every ride,

lolling dizzy on the grass with our cotton candy and lemonade and fresh doughnut holes before watching the sun set from the Ferris wheel. Yes, we can rent that speedboat and go tubing! Yes, we can spend a three-day weekend at the waterslides! Hey, did you notice that sign for U-pick raspberries, kids? Of *course* I'm turning the car around so we can fill our sun hats with the sweetest, ripest berries that we'll gorge on until our teeth are full of seeds! You want popcorn with double butter *and* Sour Patch Kids *and* those nachos with the disgusting liquid cheese that is squirted from a machine at the movie theatre? Well, obviously you do — let's go for it!

And in between the big adventures, we had little ones. He took the kids to the park to fly kites, ride bikes. He built little rockets from science kits with them, set them off in the driveway at twilight. He bought them the greatest graphic novels at the comic book store, the weirdest candy at the bulk sweets emporium, the juiciest Whopper with extra pickles at Burger King.

And now? Now they're stuck with *me*. No more magic for you, kids.

O

It is now 3:50 a.m.

I sit at the kitchen table and look at my old albums on Facebook. Me and Sam at Englishman River, smiling for a selfie, Quinn and Lark building a sandcastle in the background. At his cousin's wedding in Regina, flushed from dancing. Another pic from the same wedding, in a photo booth, Sam wearing Bullwinkle antlers for some reason, me and the kids in sequined cowboy hats, all of us grinning.

At 4:07 a.m., I decide to take off all my clothes and put
on Sam's leather jacket inside out with its skin against mine. I
stand in the dark and stare at myself in the hallway mirror, my
chubby legs white and soft as brie.

"Go fuck yourself," I say to my reflection. I dare the mirror
to break and let me through.

"You look crazy," my reflection says back.

I do look crazy. I look fucking *crazy*. My hair is a nest of
frizz, my eyes blotted with days-old black makeup, my eyelids
swollen, my tits drooping like they're trying to escape from my
chest and get away from this mess once and for all. And I am
wearing an enormous, inside-out leather jacket.

"You are really going to town right now," says my reflection.

"Well, your jacket is ugly," I say.

The jacket *is* ugly. Huge, bulky, too long. It is the ugliest
jacket that has ever happened. I never liked it on Sam, the way
it turned his silhouette instantly into one that could belong
only to a perverted game emporium nerd.

"You look like a flasher," I'd tell him.

"I look great! I love this jacket!"

I try crawling back into bed and sleeping with the jacket
still on, but inside-out leather turns out to be the opposite of
cozy, so I take it off and hang it on the closet door. But now the
moonlight is coming through the window and the jacket looks
like a giant, creepy, floating monster with no head, so I run
to the wall and flick on the lights, take the jacket and throw
it out into the hallway, and run back to my bed. I try to sleep,
but intrusive, nightmarish scenes of the Clive's Classic Lounge
night keep flashing at me. Saul's face in the car that morning,
how he looked like a captive who was about to be released,
finally, after ten years eating slop in a six-by-three vertical cell.

The humiliation of it all and how I did it to myself. Some self-care night.

Everyone runs away from you, whispers my mother, *once they get to know you.*

I try reading a book.

I cannot express it; but surely you and every-
body have a notion that there is or should be an
existence of yours beyond you. What were the
use of my creation, if I were entirely contained
here? My great miseries in this world have been
Heathcliff's miseries, and I watched and felt
each from the beginning: my great thought in
living is himself. If all else perished, and he
remained, I should still continue to be; and
if all else remained, and he were annihilated,
the universe would turn to a mighty stranger: I
should not seem a part of it. My love for Linton
is like the foliage in the woods: time will change
it, I'm well aware, as winter changes the trees.
My love for Heathcliff resembles the eternal
rocks beneath: a source of little visible delight,
but necessary. Nelly, I am Heathcliff! He's al-
ways, always in my mind: not as a pleasure, any
more than I am always a pleasure to myself, but
as my own being. So don't talk of our separation
again: it is impracticable.

Is *Wuthering Heights* a good book to read for the fifty-thousandth time after you've just been creeped out by your dead love's jacket seemingly floating in midair? I picture myself as a ghost, roaming like Cathy through the moors, except I'd roam around Quadra and McKenzie, and I'd ride a skateboard. Then I have an idea. It is a really, really good idea.

The best thing, the very best thing you could possibly do right now, I tell myself, *would be to spend the next three hours, until Benji wakes up, signing up for every single internet dating site in the whole wide world.*

Tell us a little about what you're looking for in the space below!

Looking for a basement druid person who likes making kombucha, organic gardening, and basket weaving, and yet who also makes YouTube rap videos and does penis graffiti and throws garbage in his neighbours' yard. That's not who I want to date — I just want to know if that person exists.

What about you? Tell us about yourself in the space below! Happy fishing!

I don't want to be cremated. I want to be buried in case someone ever wants to dig me up and cradle my bones. 5'7", curvy.

It's now 5:00 a.m., and I am staring at a very curious pile of crusty dishes on the counter. I don't remember using any of them. The sun is coming up. It's a pink summer morning. Birds are making bird noises; the kids will be up soon. I'm thinking about how many dead bodies I've seen, tallying them in my mind's eye, when I remember Starla and the dead woman behind the movie theatre.

I google it again. There's an update:

July 7, 2016

SAANICH — It's a mystery Saanich Police officials are still trying to solve.

A dog walker was exploring the trails behind the SilverCity Cinema the morning of December 7, 2015, when he spotted a body. The body was determined to be that of a woman in her midthirties, and her death was deemed suspicious. It's been more than six months since the woman was discovered, and officials have still been unable to locate next of kin. Her cause of death was asphyxiation, but little else is known.

The B.C. Coroners Service is turning to the public for help to find out who she was, and what happened, by releasing more details about the woman. In a news release Monday, the service and the Saanich Police asked for clues in the case.

The woman had stretch marks and a 2.7-centimetre vertical scar of unknown origin on her abdomen. She was found wearing light-blue sweatpants and a black hoodie, which was stained with a white substance later determined to be soup broth.

Anyone with information about the woman's identity is asked to contact Saanich Police.

NINE

SAM AND I WANTED TO BUY AN ACREAGE BY THE ocean. I would raise goats and write poetry; Sam would have a shop where he'd do artificial-intelligence experiments and build sentient robots. Sadly, we couldn't afford that, so we bought this half-duplex just before Benji was born. The place where Sam died, the place I still occupy and stink up with my misery.

The people who lived in the house next door to the duplex were in their nineties. We called them the Old Man and the Old Lady.

Every day, the Old Man walked down the driveway to get his mail. He had the distinctive old-man gait, entirely slow and creaking. Sometimes the Old Lady would join him. They would walk arm in arm, their terrier on his little leash all dolled up in a knitted blue vest.

The Old Lady was a round, hammy person with deep frown lines. Her hair was jet black with a shock of white at the roots. She was always wearing bright polyester muumuus and ruby lipstick, aviator sunglasses, and orthopaedic socks pulled to her knees. The Old Man's trip down the driveway was even longer when she went along because she had to stop and catch her breath every few steps.

When they got to the mailbox, they would collect their mail and then just stand there for a few minutes, looking around, like they weren't sure what was going on. And then, at exactly the same moment and without saying a word to each other, they would turn around, still arm in arm, a solemn polka in slow motion, and start their sitcom-length journey back up to the house.

"I don't like it when the Old Man looks at me," I said to Sam one day. "He just stands there in the driveway five feet away and stares at me when I'm getting the kids out of the car."

"He's just old. He's looking at you because he wants to make friends."

"Well, I don't want to be his friend. I can't help it if garbage falls out of the car when I open the doors. He shakes his head at me! I don't want an old-man friend who stares at me all the time and judges me."

Sam told me not to be silly, to just relax. "Why do you always assume that people are out to get you? Why isn't your default assumption that people are friendly and kind?"

"Because they aren't."

"The guy is two hundred years old, Elsie. He's just hoping you'll say hello to him."

The Old Man was always out in his yard, slowly raking things and pushing small piles of foliage around in a wheelbarrow. I would watch him sometimes from my kitchen window when I was making dinner.

One night in late August, I noticed the Old Man was raking fig leaves even more slowly than usual. It was as if he was pulling the rake through molasses. I took note of this but got distracted by cooking and kids, and it couldn't have been more than fifteen minutes later that somebody down there was wailing terribly and an ambulance was rolling up the Old People's driveway with no siren and no urgency.

"There's an ambulance at the Old People's house," I called to Sam, and he sauntered into the kitchen and leaned over me, saw the paramedics. The wailing was louder now, closer to our window, the rhythmic, hyperventilated sobs of mourning, that toe-crushed-with-a-hammer throbbing sound.

Sam went out on the deck to get a better look. I followed him with a half-peeled potato in my hand.

"Look," he said, "the Old Man is dead."

And he was, his body crumpled on top of a pile of brush at the trunk of a fig tree, the handle of the rake still in his palm. His green cardigan and brown pants made it so that he blended right in with the yard. And there was his wife, kneeling, a mountain of sobbing flesh rocking over her husband's smallness.

"Oh God," I said.

"He's dead as a doorknob," Sam said, lighting a cigarette and leaning over the railing for a better view. "Must've had a heart attack."

The paramedics had made their way down the sloping grass to the fig tree. One of them put his hands on the woman's shoulders, gently trying to pull her away from the body while his colleague looked for a pulse.

"I'm going inside," I said. "You should come inside, too."

"No! I can't miss this," Sam said. "I want to watch."

"Okay, fill your boots, but it doesn't seem right."

He poked his head in every minute or so to give me an update.

"They're taking the old guy's shirt off now. Why are they cutting it off? Aww, it's a sweater vest. But why are they doing that? Oh, they're going to shock his heart, I think. Why are they bothering? He's clearly long gone, so why?"

I ignored him, kept peeling the potatoes. One of the kids asked for a glass of milk. I took the roast out of the oven, washed some dishes. I was putting potatoes in the pot when Sam arrived inside and hugged my waist, kissed the back of my neck. I turned around and crossed my arms over my chest.

"I don't want to make out when you've just been watching the saddest day in the Old Lady's life," I said. "It's too sad and horrible."

"Come on, don't be so serious," Sam said. He grabbed a beer from the fridge, popped the tab, and took a long swig. "I'm going back out there. Come watch with me."

"No," I said, but I followed him out anyway, because what else was I supposed to do?

It was just about to rain, the air thick and wet and electric. Sam put his arm around my shoulder, and I leaned my head against his chest. We stood there together, watching this death that meant nothing to us.

"I feel bad for complaining that he stares at me," I said. "I actually really love it when he stares at me."

"Yeah, you should feel bad. I always said hello to him, so my conscience is clean."

One of the paramedics heard us talking, looked up at us. Sam did a sailor's salute. The paramedic saluted back.

The Old Lady's wailing had stopped. She was moaning quietly now, kneeling on all fours a few feet away from her husband's body and rocking back and forth, a hospital blanket draped over her back like she was a horse. Another ambulance arrived, and two more paramedics hopped out and meandered down the hill, snapping on their latex gloves. They made small talk with their colleagues, who pointed up at us. They all smiled and waved.

"This is weird," I said to Sam as we waved and smiled back.

The Old Man's corpse was lifted and placed inside a long, black bag on a stretcher. We were so close that we heard the zipper close.

"Do you think he knew what hit him?" Sam asked.

"I don't know," I said. "But it's kind of lovely that he was doing yardwork. He seemed to really enjoy yardwork. He was such a good guy."

"Yeah, great guy," Sam said. "Salt of the earth."

It started to rain, so I went inside, but he stayed out there, smoking one cigarette after another, totally fascinated. He had to watch all of it, he said; he had to get to the end. I fed the kids dinner. The sky was growing dark, and Sam watched the paramedics wheel the stretcher up the hill.

I was giving the baby a bath when he came inside, sat on the toilet beside me.

"She wouldn't leave the spot where he died," he said.

"Oh?"

"She was just sitting there in the pouring rain, leaning against the tree. Some middle-aged guy came and sat beside her. It must be their son."

"Yeah, probably their son."

He finished his beer and went off to the kitchen, where I heard the cupboard open and close, followed by the unmistakable sound of someone trying to swallow something quickly and quietly.

Sam did this thing sometimes, this thing where he'd drink beer openly, which was no big deal, but then sneak guzzles of the vodka he'd hidden on the top shelf of the pantry, a place he knew I couldn't reach without a stepstool. Before Benji was born, before my dad died, these furtive swigs would happen only once in a while, but after my dad's death, it became more frequent. I don't know what it was about my dad's death that made Sam's alcoholism worse.

Actually, that's a lie. I do know. It was my grief and distance that did it. But I don't like to think about that; going down that road is a recipe for What-Ifs, and if grief alone can't kill a person, the What-Ifs can. The point is that whenever Sam did the secret vodka-swigging thing, he'd seem fine one minute, playful and thoughtful and animated about whatever obsession was at the centre of his attention — a Ted Chiang story, an obscure mythic monster he'd discovered, a song — and moments later he'd be slurring, his eyes fluttering and rolling back in his head.

"It's awful seeing you like that," I'd tell him the next day. "I hate it."

He never remembered his sloppiness or any of the conversations that happened when he was sloshed, and hearing about it mortified him. He would always apologize, always insist I watch him pour his stash of vodka down the drain. "I just like to find the edge," he'd say, "but sometimes I trip and fall right off. Forgive me."

Sam's dysfunctional relationship with booze became harder to ignore as the frequency of sneaky sipping increased. When it was every three months, I could pretend we had no problems between drunken events. But there was that shift in Sam after my dad died. He was no longer trying to find the edge; he was sprinting right off it. One night, he fell down the stairs and hit his head on the banister, resulting in sixteen stitches at the base of his skull. One morning I woke up with him passed

out beside me, jacket on and socks covered in mud. He was
caked in mud from head to toe. We'd gone to sleep together in our undies, so he must have woken up, got dressed, got
drunk, found a muddy outdoor location to roll around in, lost
his shoes somehow, and made his way back to bed, all while I
was sleeping.

These events were so disturbing that I learned to retreat,
to dissociate, to become an observer rather than a participant
in what could no longer be described as anything other than
progressively serious alcoholism. I threatened to leave him, too,
of course. And in the September before he died, I did. I moved
with the kids into my friend's basement suite, determined to
show him how much he'd lose if he kept drinking like he was.
It lasted only two weeks. I was lured back with emails involving
declarations of cosmic love and promises of AA, of counselling,
of treatment. And when I went back, I reasoned that if I didn't
drink with him, if I dissociated and refused to engage with him
while he was bingeing, I wasn't an enabler, right? Right?

By the night the Old Man died, I was so practised at re-
treating that it felt like putting on well-worn chain mail. He
passed out on the couch, and I put the kids to bed alone, then
settled into the loveseat with a novel while he snored with his
baseball cap over his face. I hoped he'd sleep it off and leave me
alone. Unfortunately, his phone buzzed and woke him. He sat
up abruptly, looked around in a panic.

"I'm up!" he yelled, rubbing his eyes violently. "Am I late
for work?"

"You're not late for work. It's nine o'clock at night. It's
Saturday."

"It is?"

"Yes."

He gave a sloppy smile, sat beside me, grabbed both my hands urgently. "Put your book down," he said. He head-butted the book against my chest and tried to lay his face against my heart.

"No," I said.

His eyes were bloodshot, his face ruddy. He was so drunk he couldn't focus properly on my face.

"You're so beautiful," he said.

"I'm tired," I said.

"The Old Man didn't know he was going to die," he said.

"No," I said.

"Come to bed, darling. Come and tuck me in. Come cuddle."

I looked at him for a long time then; looked into the drunken swirls of his eyes. He looked back and blinked slowly, tried a lopsided smile.

"Bed?" he asked.

I shook my head.

He put his face in his hands and began to sob. "You don't love me anymore."

"I don't want to be around you when you're loaded, and I'm not talking about this now. Please go to bed."

"But the Old Man loved the Old Lady, and then he died," he said.

"Yes," I said, "it was sad."

"You don't love me," he said.

"Go to bed, Sam," I said. "Please. Please don't do this tonight."

He knitted his brow and looked at me searchingly. I looked back, trying not to cry, too, because my tears would be for different reasons, pointless and bottomless.

I must have looked mean, because his face hardened and his eyes narrowed.

"You're a bitch with no soul," he slurred.

"Yeah. I guess I am. Go to bed now."

He tried to manoeuvre his body up and swayed over the coffee table for a moment before falling over. Then he cleared his throat, tried to get up, and fell down again.

"I'm a good person," he said, to himself mostly, as he crawled toward a chair that he used to steady himself and stand.

He made his way down to the bedroom, slammed the door. I went back to my book.

An hour later, he appeared again in the living room.

"Hi," he said sombrely, seating himself beside me on the couch again. "What're you doing?"

"Reading."

"Put your book down," he said. Again he head-butted my book against my chest and tried to lay his face against my heart.

"No, Sam."

"You're so beautiful."

"No. No, no, no. Please."

"The Old Man —"

"Yeah, the Old Man loved the Old Lady, and then he died. You just did all of this an hour ago. You've already said all of these things."

"I did?"

"Yes, an hour ago."

"No, I didn't. I just woke up. I had a nap, and I just woke up."

"No, you said all of these things an hour ago. You're drunk, and you don't remember. And you won't remember any of this in the morning. Please, go back to bed now."

"Hey, hey hey hey, darling, hey. Can we talk about it, what's bothering you? I can tell you're mad, but I don't get it."

O

All diseases are cruel. They're all bad, callous, destructive, and ugly in their own special ways. Addiction is the same, but there's another layer to it. It's not like a psychotic disorder where a mania or psychosis renders your loved one obviously insane. No, it's far more insidious than that. The addiction is a plagiarist, and the addicted person's brain and personality are slowly, slowly, slowly overwritten with a new narrative but in the same pen. You look at your person, and they seem okay. Your brilliant, beautiful person. Your Big Love.

The plagiarist brings hors d'oeuvres and doesn't seem like a plagiarist at all. He's wearing fancy clothes and has great taste in music, and it's all so free. But there must be a bill to pay. Who's paying the bill?

Relax, he says, I've got everything covered.

After the night Sam went to sleep and didn't wake up, and after the coroner had come and gone, and after the fog of the funeral and the *I'm So Sorrys* and the care packages, those days that hemorrhaged into the twentieth, thirty-fifth, and fiftieth day, I remembered the Old Man and the Old Lady.

When I'm out on the deck, I look up the hill at the house where the Old Lady lives, widowed. Her whole life is behind her. Long marriage, children grown. She's so lucky to be in her epilogue. I watch as her son visits to bring her the mail, take out the garbage, rake the brush below the fig tree where his father died.

Did she see the paramedics at my house that day, carrying Sam out in a long, black bag?

Does she watch me and know we are connected, that the fractals of our lives have been drawn in parallel lines?

The Old Man loved the Old Lady, and then he died. He just died.

TEN

THE FIRST DEAD BODY I EVER SAW WAS MY MOTHER'S, so vandalized by cancer that her face was grotesque. Her cheekbones were Ping-Pong balls, her eyes sunken. She died with her mouth wide open, so one of my aunties put a rolled-up towel under her chin to keep it closed. That was an important thing to do, I figured, in case a little animal decided to sneak in there and build a nest.

Meanwhile, the other auntie was busy prying the rings off my mother's dead fingers. "Can't leave them on too long, Elsie. Her fingers'll puff right up!"

My grandmother sat in a chair in the corner of the room. "She was such a good girl," she was saying over and over. "Such a good, good girl."

My grandmother's name is Ada May, and since my mom died back in 2006, her brain has slowly been turning to Swiss cheese. She held on to her marbles long enough to bid farewell to her youngest daughter, and shortly thereafter the cheesing began. Her mother, Grandma K, had Alzheimer's, too.

I think about this a lot, this brain-cheesing process called Alzheimer's, mostly because I expect to follow suit one day, if I'm lucky enough to reach old age without some form of cancer snuffing me out first. And I've reached the conclusion that there is actually a beauty in forgetting. Not to diminish the pain it causes to family and friends — not at all. But for the person — for the cheese-brain — I think it is a way of getting to let go of life and all its attachments without actually having to say goodbye. It's slipping back into the void slowly, the personality dissolving at a gentle simmer, the mind drifting up into the heavens years before the body stops. The whole thing sounds pretty good to me.

Ada May is still beautiful. Some old people are decrepit, with their jowls and eyelids sagging like sideways vaginas, but not Ada May. Her cheeks are still full and pink, her lips plump, her eyes bright. It's just that now she's an old, cute baby. She doesn't remember that her husband has been dead for sixteen years — she wouldn't believe you if you told her she ever had a husband at all. She doesn't remember her brother, her parents, or falling in love, or giving birth five times or being a nurse or travelling the world or even her own middle name. But she is happy. I think she's the happiest pretty old baby I've ever seen, if not the happiest person I've ever seen. Actually, that's not true. She gets mad sometimes, mostly at the health care aides my uncle hired to feed her lunch and help her to the bathroom. Also, she's kind of a bully. She hurls books and teacups and lamps when she doesn't get her way.

I haven't seen Ada May since Sam died. She didn't come to the funeral because it would have required her to take the ferry from Vancouver, and she doesn't know what a ferry is anymore.

Sam met Ada May just once. It was right before she was totally swallowed by the Alzheimer's. We had a barbecue on my uncle's patio. I introduced her to Sam, and she sat there with her little Yorkie on her lap, wearing the same bemused and elegant expression she always had. I told her about the house we had just rented together, how it had a walk-in closet just like she and Grandpa had had in their old townhouse, how Lark loved climbing the enormous fig tree in the backyard. She nodded politely, but the comprehension was mostly gone by then.

"She's still quite beautiful," Sam said in the car on the way home.

"She is. She has kind of a timeless grace about her, doesn't she?"

"If you look like that when you're old, I'll still ravage you every day."

"I know. I'll probably look more like a confused elephant, though. Will you still love me?"

"You betcha, baby."

O

Hunting for meaning is the most natural thing to do when you're confused, and I find myself confused a lot these days. Luckily, I've learned that meaning can be found in just about anything, if I concentrate hard enough.

One trick I like is to stand in front of a bookshelf. I close my eyes and run one hand along the book spines until I get the feeling that it's time to stop. Whatever book my hand is resting on is the one I pull out. My eyes remain closed as I flip through the pages, and the sentence my index finger lands on is "The

One." It's the sentence that illuminates the meaning of the day,
a Very Special Message from the Universe to me.

Today, I pull out *Ozma of Oz*:

Finally, in despair, she decided to leave it entirely to chance.

See? Could it be any clearer?

O

There's a guy coming over this evening to talk about fixing my
overgrown disgrace of a backyard. I like its shameful appear-
ance. Starla does not. She is convinced that the three-foot-tall
weeds are attracting all the neighbourhood rats to gather and
plot against her. She keeps knocking on my door to tell me
about how the rats are all my doing and are making her afraid
to go outside.

I'm a slob, but I don't leave garbage in my yard, and I keep
the recycling inside until recycling day. The rats aren't my problem — they're not my fucking problem — and I'm getting really tired of her thinking up ways to get me to take responsibility
for her rodent prejudice.

"They're not my rats," I told her for the hundredth time when
she banged on my door like a cop at eight the other morning. I'd
answered groggy and confused. "I don't have pet rats," I said.

"Well," she said, "I went into your yard when you were at
work, and I could see their little trails through the weeds you're
growing back there. They're getting through the fence into my
yard, and I need you to take care of it."

"I like my yard natural, and dandelions are important for the
bees, but I'll cut them down if it would make you feel better."

"Thanks. It would."

I called my sister to complain.

"My neighbour is being fucking crazy again. She's convinced I'm breeding rats over here."

"Just get the yard cleaned up, Elsie. It's got to get done anyway if you're going to sell the place. I know a guy; I'll text you his email."

"Oh, so should I shave my armpits, too, if Starla thinks they're attracting rats?"

"Your yard is a jungle — come on."

"It is not! It's a garden of common weeds and grasses — a garden, not a jungle."

"Just call the guy, Elsie. His name is Trevor. He's good. Anyways, I've gotta go. I'll text you."

"Fine."

She said she would text me, so I was expecting a text, but after twenty minutes of waiting and seething over Starla basically saying that I'm a disgusting rat person, I decided to do something useful.

I found a piece of construction paper and made a flyer, which I folded up and placed in Starla's mailbox:

> To: Starla
> From: The Rat King
> Where: Next door
> When: Now (or whenever)
> RSVP: YES

On the inside, I drew a little picture of a friendly rat with an eye patch and sharp fangs, and a text bubble saying *YOU ARE INVITED TO RAT WORLD!* Underneath that I listed some of the best things about Rat World:

- Lots of garbage to eat!
- Mazes! Prizes!
- Rats! Rats! Rats! Rats galore!
- Disease-friendly! Free hugs and kisses!

Trevor the Yard Guy arrives with a clipboard and a measuring tape, his jeans secured with a belt high above his belly button, his T-shirt tucked tight. He is a tall and tidy man with a crushing handshake and teeth like yellow coral, and he is currently tromping around my yard, looking at things. He keeps saying *you guys*, as in, *you guys* could get some landscaping rocks, *you guys* could save some money by filling this area with gravel, *you guys* should try power-washing this patio.

Once it's time to talk money, he seems nervous to be throwing numbers around. He keeps glancing over at the back door of my house, as though he expects a hairy husband to burst out and yell, *Hey, that's a rip-off! You trying to rip off my wife?*

I tell him I'd like to book right away, hoping that nailing down a date will help him feel less squirrelly, but nope, he's still being all weird and looking at the door.

"I'll just leave the quote with you and let you guys discuss it — how's that?"

"I'd like to just book it now."

"You don't want to discuss it with your husband?" *Bam —* there it is.

"No. Can we just book a date now, please?"

It's not computing; I can see him short-circuiting.

"I'm seeing a lot of toys in the yard," he says, trying out loud to make sense of this crazy puzzle. "You have kids obviously, eh? I just thought —"

"Yeah. Single mum."

"Oh, okay. Well, this'll be a good deal for you, then, eh?"

He scratches out his quote and replaces it with one for fifty bucks less. "My wife's ex is a real piece of work, eh? Gives me grief all the time, and it's been five years. I hope your ex is treating you right."

"He treats me great."

"Oh, good to hear."

"He died last Christmas."

"Aw, jeez. I'm sorry."

"It's okay. Dead people are nice. They always treat you right."

He grimaces, then nods earnestly like we're at church and I've just quoted some Bible passage that stabbed him right in the Christ bone. I'm really expecting him to flip open his calendar and pencil me in now, but he doesn't; the idea of the dead husband has relaxed him, and he sits down in a patio chair, leans forward with his elbows on his knees and hands clasped, and looks at me mournfully. It's a look that says, *Baby, we've known each other for a few months now, and it's about time we had a little talk about us.*

"Look, I'm gonna be real with you for a minute," he says. "It's crazy that you're going through all this. It's a crazy coincidence, eh? 'Cause I'm having a real hard time right now, too, so I know what you're going through."

"Oh?"

"Yeah. My dog just died of cancer. We tried to save him, but there wasn't nothing we could do, eh? Twelve years old. Just had to let him go."

"That's awful."

His eyes are welling with tears.

I sit down in the chair beside him, and we gaze at the weeds together.

"Yup, nothing fair about it. He was my best bud. And me and the wife are going through some stuff right now too, because 'course, whenever it rains, it pours. Wife's mom's in the hospital because she fell off a stool and hit her head, so that's real hard because now we gotta visit every day. And then my dad, Christ. He just had a hip replacement, and the food in the hospital is so bad it almost poisoned him to death, and we had to bring in A&W every day, eh?"

"Man. Yeah, that's a lot. Sorry about your dog."

Trevor says his dog, ZZ Top Dog, was a beauty, just a beauty of a boy, eh? A mutt with a heart of gold who could open the fridge with his paws and help himself to whatever food he wanted. ZZ Top Dog danced, too — did I ever meet a dog who danced?

"No, never."

"Yup, he danced all right. To the beat and everything."

Trevor also tells me that 2016 has been a real bad year for a lot of people.

"Real bad year," he says. "Something's in the water, eh?"

"Yeah, in the water."

"I'm always delighted to hear that a lot of other people are having a bad year," I say.

We settle on a date, and he talks a bit more about his dad and the hospital food. Then he stands up and vigorously brushes some invisible sawdust off his pants. "Gotta go pick up the wifey now."

"Okay. Thanks for coming."

He offers his hand for another shake. I take it. It is uncomfortable. It goes on far too long, it's too tight, and he's looking deep into my soul, smiling intensely with those yellow teeth.

"Nice meeting you, Elsie."

"Nice meeting you, too."

He climbs into his white utility van. It doesn't have windows in the back.

I feed the kids a frozen pizza. In the living room after eating, Lark performs a dance she learned at school, and I pretend very hard to seem interested, which is difficult.

My children have become blurs that squawk and orbit around me making demands, and even though I don't fully see them anymore, I respond as though I do. Still, I have the sneaking suspicion that they're the only things tethering me to the Earth.

I make it through the bedtime routine. Somehow I've done that every night since Sam died. The muscle memory of parenthood — baths, storytimes, forehead kisses. Then I settle into my insomnia routine of blasting Sam's favourite songs in my headphones, pacing the house, yelling at him, smoking cigarettes, and crying.

I fall asleep at 3:45 a.m. and dream of Trevor the Yard Guy. I am floating through the underground parking lot of the SilverCity Cinema when I see him unloading something from the back of his van into a wheelbarrow. It is a human body wrapped in a blue camping tarp, tied up with rope. I know it's a human body because I can see the hair, matted and dark. ZZ Top Dog is there, sniffing things like a good boy and following along as Trevor wheels the body into the forest behind the theatre. He dumps it in a small, marshy clearing, then he looks at the sky.

"It wasn't me," he whimpers. "I just found her that way."

O

From: Elsie J. <Elsiejane@vergemail.com>
Date: September 16, 2011 at 2:35 p.m.
Subject: Re: easy to love
To: Sam <QBit_Sam@vergemail.com>

I have to tell you something: I am interested in robots in a sexual way. I'm not just saying that to be an adorable oddball. You sent me that monkey/prosthetics article and I got so turned on thinking about robot sex that I had to masturbate twice in the library bathroom and I'm not kidding. I was there to pick up a couple of parenting books, on my lunch break, and that made it extra inappropriate.

Remember that geminoid robot video we watched a couple weeks ago? I was thinking about the potential merger of those two technologies: the monkey prosthetics and the geminoid. Like a quadriplegic man being able to get kinetic with his wife by puppeteering his own personalized robot version of himself. There is something creepy and romantic there, but not creepy in a perv way, creepy in an otherworldly, astonishing, thrilling, and still very very sad but beautiful way. I honestly cannot think of anything hotter than Christopher Reeve sitting in his electro chair and watching his robot brain puppet go to town on his wife.

I just realized that Christopher Reeve and his wife are both dead and I'm a colossal asshole. Forget Christopher Reeve. No, don't forget him — never forget. Fuck it, let's use him. Christopher Reeve, our actor, able to control the handsome, robust, fully functional Superman-era robot version of himself with his thoughts, to make and watch it do all the things he used to love to do when he had feeling. He can ravage his wife with his mind, just go bananas on her body, and even though he still can't feel a thing, he can know he is making her feel something. The frustration and the longing there, it's beautiful. And it's fucking hot. And I am such a bad person. Is it sadistic to get turned on by this? I don't think I'm a sadist. It's romantic, right? Isn't it? I can't help it, I really can't help but think it is the most sensual, sad, romantic scenario I've stumbled upon in weeks. It's so beautiful!

I think I must be a really messed-up asshole, though, actually. Because when I really stop to consider what I just wrote, I realize that if I were the paralyzed person and you were the object of my brain puppet's lust, I would become jealous of my brain puppet eventually for getting to touch you. I really would. And I'd get so frustrated that I would make my puppet punch itself in the face. So I'm not a sadist or a masochist, I'm just an asshole.

What if you got so mad at your puppet that you made it pour boiling water over its head? Then you would watch its face melt and its circuit board fry, and it would be like watching your own face melting and the frying circuit board would be your soul frying and you would be overcome with sadness, pity, and regret. No. I'm done with this whole fantasy now.

We're still skiing next weekend? I need to borrow a snowsuit from someone. I'm excited!

I love you.

-Elsie

ELEVEN

I AM HAPPY TO REPORT THAT MY SLEEPLESS ONLINE dating/Sam email hobby is going very well. And by that, I mean it's going terribly. The void left by Sam is a very specific one that can be filled only by a second soulmate, or at least a handsome, roguish weirdo like Saul who can keep me entertained. I'm only thirty-four years old, so I'm doing what I have to do to survive, okay? Everyone should be proud of me that I have a date tonight.

The fact that I still have to show up for work every morning at eight is a bit annoying, especially since I need to prepare myself to meet my sequel soulmate tonight.

I'm pretty sure my co-workers have noticed that I'm not brushing my hair and I smell like I haven't showered in a week. It's not that I don't care about personal hygiene, it's just that I'm so in my head that I keep forgetting it's in a body, and every ounce of outward-focused energy I have goes to making sure my kids are fed and clean and clothed.

I've taken to using old perfume samples in my armpits instead of deodorant, which I dab on in the car at red lights. It doesn't quite cover the B.O., but it reminds me of Ada May, who always gave me a little plastic baggie full of samples from the Estée Lauder counter. I kept them in the middle console of my car for years, never suspecting that they'd come in so handy.

I'm feeling pretty good about this date tonight. It's with a man I would like to call the Cabin Builder. I call him that because he is building a cabin, you see — a *cabin!* A cabin in the middle of nowhere, because that is what tortured men do when they're all out of luck and just need to find the right broad to get their blood running hot enough to return to the din and buzz of the real world. He has a son, he says, and his son likes collecting car magazines and socializing with friends, which he finds confusing and unrelatable, since he is more into reading, building his cabin, solitude, and more cabin-building. *Swoon.* He says he likes Raymond Carver and Kurt Vonnegut and Joanna Newsom, which all bode well for replacement soulmate status.

The Cabin Builder and I are about to meet right here in Bastion Square, where I am currently seated on a bench in front of the Maritime Museum, so excited and nervous that my panties are soaking through my skirt onto the bench.

In his profile pics, the Cabin Builder appeared strapping and subtly tortured. He had some furrowed angsty brows — just how I like 'em — with a big old black beard, unruly hair, and sunburned arms. He was even holding an axe in one pic, which meant he had just been chopping wood, which meant he loved to build fires, which meant he was strong, sensitive, and could be my guide through the wilderness of forests and life.

He also looked like he might be able to stare into a wolf's eyes and speak to the wolf telepathically.

He's late. It's busy downtown, and I can tell that everyone who walks past me knows I am waiting to meet someone from the internet. My phone is dead, so I keep busy by texting an imaginary friend on the black screen. In fact, I am texting Sam, so the black screen is perfect.

> Hello, Sam, hello! Yes, it is I, Elsie. Yes, yes, still incarcerated here on Earth, and in fact I am texting to you from the escarpment of an internet date which I set up in order to redirect my neurosis from one point of focus to another. I am wearing your favourite lipstick, LOL. Write back.

When the Cabin Builder walks up, the setting sun is behind him, and his silhouette appears very pleasant. But then he gets closer, and I recognize him, but barely. It's like the opposite of how you vaguely recognize your grandparents in younger pictures of themselves. I can tell he was once the strapping wolf-whisperer from his pictures, but something has happened to him since then. Something terrible, sad, and soul-sucking. I have never seen a sadder-looking man. He reaches his hand out for a shake, and I take it, and it's dry, limp, devoid of energy. We do the hello, hello, how are you, good good, good good.

"So what do you want to do," he says flatly.

I suggest we find somewhere to get a coffee.

"I thought we would walk around first and talk," he says.

We walk around the inner harbour. I ask him what's big in his life.

"Well, I'm mostly just building my cabin," he says.

I ask about the cabin.

"I'm building it myself," he says. *I'm a big boy. I'm building a big-boy cabin.*

We walk in silence for several minutes.

"So where are we going?" I ask.

"We're walking around," he says. Then he tries a smile. It almost cracks his face. It looks painful.

"Let's go in there," I say.

We go in there. It is a generic hipster bar with shared long tables. We settle in across from each another a few feet down from a couple who is clearly madly in love, all kisses and googly eyes.

He orders a beer; I get water.

"So, you like Joanna Newsom?"

"Some of it."

"Oh. What's your favourite album?"

"Well, I'm building my cabin right now, and I don't have a lot of time to listen to music. I can't remember her right now; I would have to go on YouTube."

"Oh, don't you have a CD player or a radio at your cabin?"

"No. There's no electricity. It's very remote where I'm building my cabin."

He is building his cabin in Deadman Falls. I'm not making that up. He tells me all about it: how he bought a new truck and then had to take it back to the dealership to get a longer bed so that he could transport more materials. This is a good five-minute monologue with many other details about wood stuff that you buy for building cabins, roads with potholes, and trim levels in trucks.

I ask him what he does when he's back in Victoria, visiting his kid.

"Not much. I'm unemployed right now, but I do make sculptures."

"Oh! Cool. What kind of sculptures?"

"You'd have to see them to understand."

"Oh, okay. So, like, abstract?"

"No. They're concrete."

"Oh, made of concrete, you mean?"

"They're made of wood."

"Ah. Like your cabin."

"Maybe you can come over after this and I'll show them to you."

Oh yeah, I say, that'd be great, it's just that I only have a babysitter for another half-hour. Darn it anyway.

I get a ride home in his truck. He pulls a CD of Rod Stewart doing jazz standards from his glovebox. Puts it in, turns it up nice and loud.

"I'm just left on Poppy Avenue here."

I thank him for the ride.

"Can I text you?" he asks.

"For sure!" I say.

I pay the babysitter. Then I write an email to a friend that says, *I just went on the best date with the most handsome, interesting, wonderful man. There really are plenty of fish! I can't wait to experience all the wonderful surprises life has in store for me!* And then I cry until my nose is so full of snot that I can't breathe, which I find so ridiculous that I began to laugh and spray it everywhere. I go to the bathroom and examine my face, my red nose, my puffy eyes, all the new wrinkles that have drawn themselves on since Sam died. There is eye makeup running down my cheeks. I put more dots of mascara under my eyes and rub them with water for added tragic effect.

Sam told me once that he had a fetish for girls crying with mascara running down their faces.

"How do you like that?" I say to the air.

Sexy as fuck, you crazy bitch, he says.

Sexy as fuck.

○

Sam proposed when I was pregnant with Benji.

I was in a restless sleep, my hips aching and a pillow between my thighs. The lights came on and I sat up, bleary-eyed, to find Sam kneeling beside the bed, a ring between his thumb and finger. He didn't even ask. He just said, "Marry me, darling."

"Are you drunk?"

"Yeah, I was nervous, so I had a bottle of wine."

The ring was an opal encircled with teeny diamonds. It was the most beautiful thing I'd ever seen. It looked like a cutting from the universe, like those galaxies with all the blues and purples and fire.

The week before he died, I looked at my ring while I was in the shower. Half of the opal was gone. It was like someone had taken a tiny hammer and ice pick to it, this jagged cut all the way through the middle, with only blackness left on one side. One day the opal was whole, and the next it was half. How does half a universe just disappear? If that wasn't foreshadowing, I don't know what is. Was the universe giving me other clues then too that I ignored?

I refer to Sam as my husband now, but we never got married. *My dead boyfriend* sounds awful; *my dead baby daddy* sounds worse. He is both of those things, but when speaking about his death and my status as the living half of a couple, I prefer *widow*.

Besides, we were engaged. We were planning the wedding, and it would have happened were it not for the pesky death of the groom.

I've never been to one, but I'm pretty sure from watching *Inside Edition* that ghost weddings have been done before and are relatively easy to pull off. All you do is plan the wedding, and the wedding party will show up, dead and alive, like in *Field of Dreams* but with a groom and parents instead of baseball players. Because fuck it, I said *yes* to getting married. I never agreed to cancel my wedding, and I still want to marry Sam, so I'm going to. All of our friends and family will be there, and the aisle will be a path of candles and lit pumpkins winding through a forest of arbutus and Garry oaks to the beach in Tofino. The bats and deer will say hooray as I glide down the beach in my lovely dress made of spider silk, half-galaxy and half-black, all glittery and fine. My ghost father will be there beside me in his '80s corduroy suit, and he will walk me gently forward while my ghost mother dabs the tears away, so proud and tender. And at the end of the aisle, Sam will be there in his rumpled wedding suit, his beard all black and wild, his eyes all fire. And I will say my vows to him, my invisible man, my tragic poet, my scientist, my lover, my ghost. And the stars will clap, and the band will play, and we will feast and dance into the night.

Won't you join us?

Space limited. RSVP.

○

From: Sam <QBit_Sam@vergemail.com>

Date: May 31, 2013 at 12:41 a.m.

Subject: Re: tulip bulbs

To: Elsie J. <Elsiejane@vergemail.com>

Thank you for finally replying. I understand you've been busy, but I know you've been avoiding me. And to answer your question: no. Why would you suggest that? Sure, I drink sometimes. I like it, and a couple beers after work isn't alcoholism. You have to understand that I'm in the habit of dealing with stress privately. I feel my stress as a nuisance; I'm not accustomed to having a partner in it. I do want to share, with you. But you might have to show me how. You might have to tell me it's okay, rather than suggesting I go on some kind of navel-gazing "journey," for the sake of self-knowledge, without you.

Please trust me, that I am prepared to deal with my stress with you beside me, and that I don't need time to myself, though I do appreciate that you are trying to be sensitive, and not cruel. I understand you need more time to yourself, right now, and I don't want to interfere with that. But I need to make sure that's all it is, that it's not you running, from me. At the same time, I think a relationship, any relationship, is composed of distraction, and then re-realization of each other. I come home, to you. I guess the fact that I'm writing this way means we're not done falling in love, yet. When we stop talking like this, writing like this, we'll know that we have reached the finish line. We will get there, if you want to. Only if you want to. I do. My every thought returns to you, Elsie Jane.

-Sam

TWELVE

YOU KNOW WHAT MY EVERY THOUGHT RETURNS TO? The dead woman behind SilverCity Cinema. I keep dreaming of her. Last night she was in the ground, and I was on my hands and knees digging like a frenzied dog until I found her, bloated and purple, streaked with earth, her eyes lifeless marbles of milky blue. I slung her over my shoulder and made my way out of the woods, but then she started to fall apart. An arm fell first, then a leg, but I kept trudging along until I found my car in the underground lot. I put her in the driver's seat and got in beside her, turned the keys in the ignition.

"Drive!" I commanded.

Her head swivelled and wobbled and crunched to look at me. The flesh of her chin was black with decay that had eaten through her bottom lip. She went to open her mouth to speak, but her lower jaw fell off and landed in the middle console. Her tongue quivered in her open throat like a salted slug, and she looked at me with pleading eyes.

I can't do it, her spirit said to mine.

"I said drive, you stupid bitch!"

○

When a person wakes up from a nightmare, the best thing for them to do is either read celebrity gossip websites or write a song, so I try reading about the tragic demise of Brangelina, but it makes me sad, so I pull out my guitar and my notebook to finish a little ballad I've been working on called "Dirty Little Tricks."

It goes like this:

Dirty little tricks, sad and unkind
I must have done a lot of wrong to get this dirty
     mind
What ended with a funeral started with a kiss
How else do you think a woman winds up crazy
     like this?

I record myself on my phone, throw it up on SoundCloud. Then I write a post on Facebook that says, *Hello friends! Please take a moment to listen to this cheerful and uplifting ballad! Like and subscribe!*

It's 2:47 a.m. when I post the song, and by 3:02 a.m. I have my first comment. *Well,* writes my mom's old officemate Joan, *good for you for being creative after the loss of your partner!* The comment annoys me. Joan doesn't know anything about me beyond the fact that I used to sit on my backpack as a teenager, scowling and listening to Bob Dylan on my Discman while I waited for my mom to get off work. Who does she think she is, listening to my song on Facebook when she's supposed to be sleeping like all the other seventy-year-olds?

Thank you very much, Joan, I write back, *but this song is actually about my dead cat.*

My cat is dead, but it's been about two years now. Her name was Ruby, and once upon a teenage time, I adopted her from the SPCA. I liked her because she was sitting in the back of the kennel, looking imperious while her orange siblings stuck their paws through the cage, all desperate for love. Desperation is never attractive, not even in kittens. Anyway, I loved Ruby the best I could. I gave her baths, brushed her fur, made her crowns of chained daisies. I swaddled her like an infant and sang to her, read her original poetry, flossed her teeth. We were connected, she and I, a string of love threading through our hearts. If I was upset, she'd jump on my chest and soothe me with chirps, press her forehead against mine.

Ruby. The sweetest and most beautiful cat that ever was.

"I hate that fucking cat," Sam would say. Ruby was already old when we met, and she became more senile by the day. I tried explaining things to Sam, how she was actually the sweetest cat alive, but he didn't understand. Eventually I had to admit that the dignified, emotionally attuned cat of yore was gone, replaced with a bony, lizard-eyed creature who spent her life stalking Sam around the house with a constant drone of croaky meows. As soon as Sam came along, she had no use for me anymore; she wanted only him. To meow at him. To meow and meow for no reason, to sit at his feet, to lie on his face in the night and to lick his toes with her cold morning tongue until he woke kicking and yelling, *NO! NO, NOT AGAIN, FUCK!*

The harder she wanted him, the more he despised her.

"Why can't she leave me alone?"

"She loves you. She wants to be close friends with you."

"I can't wait until she dies. She's a horrible little animal."

Benji was two weeks old, and I was nursing him in the kitchen when I looked out the window and saw a mound of calico fur in the corner of the yard.

She was still alive, but one of her cheeks was abscessed. She'd been in a fight with something — another cat, a raccoon maybe. I picked her up and could smell the infection, sweet and fetid. She was limp. She stared into my eyes.

I called Sam, sobbing. He was on his way home from work anyway, so I met him in the driveway with the baby and the dying cat in my arms.

In the waiting room of the Saanich Animal Hospital, I held her, rocked her gently, sang her Joni Mitchell songs while the other patrons side-eyed me and shifted in their seats. But she loved it. Ruby always loved my singing.

In the examination room, the vet took a deep whiff of her face.

"Smell that?" he asked.

We nodded.

He explained things. This was an eighteen-year-old cat, blah blah blah, cats don't live forever blah, intravenous antibiotics would cost $1,200 for the blah blah and the blah blah blah, and she would probably die anyway.

Sam tried to contain his glee, but it was all over his face. He was delighted that this day had finally come.

The needle was big.

Ruby wasn't scared at all. She just wanted to look at me. She was calm, resigned to her fate.

It is time, said her heart to mine. *Let me go now.*

I can't, said my heart. *I need to believe that some cats do live forever.*

As the vet approached with the put-down medicine, I backed away and held onto Ruby.

"Do you want me to hold her?" Sam asked.

I nodded. He took her out of my arms. She turned her head so she could still see me. In went the needle.

Her pupils grew wide as the opiates flooded her. "*No*," I whispered. I looked at Sam.

His eyes were firehouse red, his chin quivering.

"I'm sorry," he said. Then he looked down at Ruby, kissed the tip of her nose. "Goodnight, sweet girl," he said.

I cried the whole way home. I cried the whole evening and all through the night and Sam held my head against his chest and whispered, "Shhhhhh, shhhhhhhh, it's okay, it's okay. Everybody dies, darling. She just went to sleep."

"I should have held her," I sobbed over and over. "I'm a coward. I let her down. You shouldn't have held her when she died. You hated her."

"Yeah, I kind of did. But I might miss her."

"No, you won't."

"No, I won't. But you will. And I'm sorry. Shhhhh, don't cry."

O

After we put Ruby down, we brought her home in a cardboard box provided by the animal hospital. The plan was to bury her in the backyard, but when Sam tried to dig a hole, we discovered that it would be impossible — the soil wasn't soil at all; it was rock.

"Let's just take her back to the vet and get her cremated," I said. "This is morbid."

"I'm not paying a hundred and fifty bucks for them to spend three minutes baking her in the oven," Sam said. "No fucking way."

The compromise was that we would hike into the woods at Mount Douglas Park and bury her there. It was pouring rain. We pulled into the parking lot, which was empty. It was dinner hour. Benji was strapped to my chest in a carrier, and my umbrella was being pounded as we hiked into the brush.

Sam had a shovel in one hand and the box with the dead cat in the other, his raincoat soaked by the time he located an appropriate spot for the grave.

"This spot looks nice," I said. It was a natural divot in the ground beside the thick and ancient stump of a nursing tree.

"Okay, let's do this."

He tried to dig. He tried and tried, but he couldn't get the shovel in deep enough; the bed of the forest was too wet and packed with rocks and old roots.

"This is gonna work!" he said.

"I don't want to do this anymore," I said. "We're going to get arrested."

We had already been through this fight. I'd said it was illegal to bury your pets in provincial parks; Sam said who cares. Now he was determined to prove that it could be done. I stood there for half an hour watching him sweat and swear at his shovel as the rain came down harder and harder.

When the baby woke up and started to cry, Sam was so irritated that he threw the shovel across the forest.

"Fuck this!" he said. "Fuck that cat!"

"What? Fuck you!" I said. I grabbed the box and stomped back to the car. It was locked. My fury rose, standing in the rain with a box of cat and my baby damp and screaming. I marched back into the woods, found Sam leaning against a tree, smoking a cigarette.

"You're smoking a cigarette? Are you kidding me? I'm locked out of the car, you asshole."

"Oh, now I'm an asshole? I just spent the last hour trying to give your stupid cat a dignified burial, and you're going to call me an asshole?"

"Yes!"

"Take some pills, Elsie. You're insane."

We drove home in silence. When we pulled into the driveway, Sam stayed in the car with the engine running.

"What are you doing?" I asked him.

"Give me the box. I'm taking the cat to get cremated. Now are you happy?"

"Yes."

"Good."

In retrospect, the fights we had were as beautiful as any of Sam's sweet love letters. The quiet intensity of his gathering anger, the way he held it patiently in his mouth for hours before letting me have it in logical, poetic bursts of rage.

I wonder what he was thinking that day, driving to the animal crematorium with Ruby in the cardboard box beside him. If someone had told him that he was not long for this world either, if they had shown him a picture of himself in the morgue at the Royal Jubilee Hospital, one eye open and one closed, the trickles of dried blood under his nose, would he have believed it?

When people ask me how he died, I tell them it was a cardiac arrest. Nobody questions this — most people accept it as synonymous with *heart attack*. Do people really want to hear the truth? I'm sure some do. It's salacious, isn't it, when

someone dies before their time. I think of Joan, all the Joans of
the world, and how they talk to each other.

Was it suicide? Or drugs? An overdose?

Overdose. That's what I heard.

I wonder if she knew, the partner ...

How could she not have known? She must have known. Of
course she did.

It's the children I really feel sorry for.

Yes, those poor children.

THIRTEEN

THE SECOND DEAD BODY I EVER SAW WAS AN OVER-dose in a bedbug-infested motel room. I was there to deliver medications and a frozen meal, back in my mental health–worker days. The man didn't die from hard drugs; he died from mouth-wash. Did you know this is a way some humans die? Well, it is. Regular booze got too expensive for this poor fellow, so he resorted to shoplifting Listerine from Walmart and guzzling it until his body couldn't take a single drop more of minty freshness.

I found him in the bathroom. Full rigor mortis, his back broken over the lip of the bathtub. The sink was running water so hot that the room was full of steam, Listerine particles dancing in the air. His hands were like claws. I drove home from my shift that night and "Rocket Man" was playing on the radio, so I blasted it and sang at the top of my lungs.

Do you know what's funny about having spent ten years as a mental health worker? I never went on stress leave, not once, not even when confronted with the ugliest and most dreadful examples of human suffering. I guess I was able to distance myself from the clients, to draw a boundary between their tragedies and my heart. That's a lot harder to do with your own tragedy. When it's your own tragedy, other people draw boundaries around you. Which is why I'm on stress leave now, I think?

I would like to tell you the stress leave was entirely my choice, but I'm still a bit confused about it.

Last week, my boss caught me crying in the bathroom and called me into her office.

"Elsie, close the door. Have a seat."

"Thanks. Am I in trouble?"

"Not at all. You doing okay?"

"Oh yeah, I'm great."

"Are you sleeping at all?"

"I mean, no. But a few hours a night, so that's good. Anyway, I've finished up the Calder file, so that's good. And I'll put it in the mail today, so that's good. And I got findings back from the Singh file, so that's good."

"Yeah, that's good, Elsie. That's all great, but let's not worry about files right now, okay?"

"Why?"

"Listen, I know this job is important to you."

"Are you firing me?"

"No!"

"So what's this about?"

"Elsie, you're a great member of the team, and we all care about you, but you've been spending a *lot* of time crying in the bathroom. You were away from your desk for two hours this morning."

"I wasn't crying, actually, I was just thinking about something sad and crying in my mind, so maybe some of it came out of my mouth, ha ha!"

"Look, grief is serious. You've been through a lot."

"But I want to do a good job. I *care*."

"I know you do. But you can't do a good job when you're clearly not sleeping and you can't concentrate."

"Yes, I can. I have ADHD. I'm great at multi-tasking, so I can grieve *and* do my work *and* not sleep at the same time, so ..."

"You came back too fast after Sam died."

"I was multi-tasking."

"You need more time."

"No, I don't."

"You *need* more time. I'm wearing my social worker hat right now, not my manager hat, okay? We have benefits for these circumstances. That's what they're for."

I cried then, in front of my boss, a big dumb moose cry. Not because I felt seen or relieved or grateful for the kindness, but because I felt a crushing mix of humiliation and resentment toward Sam for turning me into this fucking *creature* who needed to be spoken to so gently.

"You think I'm doing a bad job?"

"No, you're not doing a bad job. I know the quality of your work when you're not stressed. But ... you've been *extremely* stressed. Look, this isn't me forcing you to do anything, but if it was me, I would take the time. Take care of yourself, and your kids, and get some proper rest."

Now, of course, after only a week away from the hustle of the office, I realize that it's an actual miracle I made it through eight months of full-time work while sleeping only three hours a night. How did I do that?

My lack of sleep isn't solely due to insomnia, by the way, in case you thought so. Mostly it is, but not always. Benji is a terrible sleeper. He often wakes up to nurse and then play or scream for a few hours in the early morning. Sometimes he wakes up Lark, too, and I have to settle her back to sleep. After getting them settled, I *can't* just go back to bed; I have to pace and obsess over Sam and his emails, the dead woman behind SilverCity Cinema, the debacle with Saul, and then I get to feeling so lonely and unlovable and insane that the only reasonable thing to do is set up more dates from the internet.

There is one great thing about stress leave, which is that I no longer have to rush my children in the morning. No more *Get your goddamn shoes on!*, no more dabbing perfume in my pits and scrambling to cover my dark eye bags with concealer at red lights. Now I can roll out of bed and deliver my children to summer camp, looking like the sasquatch that I am, wearing my same favourite blue sweatpants and old T-shirts with ramen stains every single day, just like the Lord intended. And after morning drop-offs, I can come home, crawl into bed, masturbate furiously, and then set up five hours of murder podcasts and go to sleep until pickup time.

I've discovered that whenever I fantasize about making love with Sam, I cry, but when I think about Saul and how he would shove me back on the bed and yank down my pants and snarl *I'm gonna eat your pussy*, I come like it's Christmas, so that's another big learning I've done so far on stress leave.

I feel like a bum, but I'm so, so tired. I'm beginning to suspect this is the kind of fatigue that no amount of sleep will fix, but I'm determined to keep trying.

Today, though? Today I'm getting dressed in real-person clothing because I'm meeting a man named Thomas (c/o Plenty of Fish) at Browns Socialhouse by Walmart — his suggestion for an elegant afternoon date.

I don't have the resolve to look nice today. I put on dirty pants and a clean shirt, smear some blush on my cheeks and some mascara on my lashes, and it's showtime.

Thomas arrives drenched in so much cologne that I'm sure he's just unscrewed the cap and dumped the whole bottle down his chest.

He's slightly elfin. Handsome.

He orders a beer for himself and one for me without asking, which is great since I do truly appreciate not having to think or make choices, especially lately, and he speaks with a lisp, which is obviously adorable on anyone.

He's nice, this Thomas. Funny, intelligent, thoughtful in his questions, insightful in his comments. There is absolutely nothing wrong with him. But ten minutes in, I want out. I want to grab my purse, plunk down my beer money, and run.

I am trying to pay attention to the content of his speech while scolding myself for dragging him out on a date that I don't even want, that I've set up only because I was lonely, bored, and heartbroken.

"I alwayth thay, don't make me the project-manager, behind-the-theenes guy — make me the prethentation guy, right? I mean, I'm pretty, right?"

"Obviously."

I want to say, look, guy, I'm so sorry for wasting your time, but I'm in love with someone else, and I made a mistake coming here. Instead, I agree that if he's hungry, he should definitely order a pizza, and I sit through three or four more stories about how he is too pretty to be doing the administrative work that is the main part of his job.

"Can I walk you to your car?"

"Sure."

He goes in for the hug, and I stiffly oblige.

"I'm not going to kith you," he says. "Not thith time, anyway. Nexth time? Can there be a nexth time?"

"Um, I'm really flaky and emotionally damaged, so I'm not sure at this moment."

It doesn't scare him off. When I get home, he's already messaged me. I delete it.

You are a terrible, terrible person for trying to use human beings as Band-Aids, hisses my mother as I toss and turn in bed. *Shame on you!*

"Like you were any different," I hiss back.

I fall asleep and wake up sucking my thumb, just in time to pick up the kids.

○

From: Sam <QBit_Sam@vergemail.com>

Date: October 26, 2011 at 12:43 p.m.

Subject: Draining the pool

To: Elsie J. <Elsiejane@vergemail.com>

What a devastating end, for that client you found. It's so sad. I'm glad you told me, though I'm sorry you have to witness such things in the course of your work. Alcoholism is a brutal affliction. The sallow cheeks and shrunken body you described, it's from malnourishment. I know you know that, but it always astounds me, how far the brain will go in pursuit of a substance that destroys the body. Booze ruins the appetite but keeps the blood sugar high, which is a pretty bad combo. If you want to drink yourself to death, you should eat your veggies to reduce the harm. One thing I'll never understand is why some people's brains get pickled, whereas others can be drunk for decades straight and still function cognitively. I wonder what their secret is. I probably don't need to know.

Tom Waits was a terrible alcoholic. I think he got sober back in 1993, in his mid-40s. It seems like a lot of creatives come to believe they need booze to make cool stuff. Tom definitely had that belief, but he overcame it. I dug up this quote from a magazine about it:

> For a while, Waits had that fear himself, the fear that when he finally dried out the songs would dry up, too. He worked through it, though. "I was trying to prove something to myself, too," he says, revealingly. "It was like, 'Am I genuinely eccentric? Or am I just wearing a funny hat?' All the big questions come up when you get sober. 'What am I made of? What's left when you drain the pool?'"

He's created a lifetime's worth of brilliant songs since he got sober. So I guess there was something left when he drained the pool, after all.

-Sam

FOURTEEN

GRIEF AND THE SPECIAL AGONY OF UNREQUITED lust are not so different from each other. The main ingredients of both are honey and hellfire. These are the substances responsible for that heavy feeling in your chest when you're in the thick of pointless yearning.

Luckily, there is a simple, three-step plan for extracting your person from such a sad state of affairs. Three things — three simple things! — that every soul must do when they find themselves questioning their worth and worthiness:

- Grab life by the pussy.
- Throw off the chains of love that bind you.
- Declare yourself free.

In a rather unexpected burst of energy this morning, I write these three things on my mirror with lipstick, only I spell the word *pussy* with four or five extras of the letter *S*, plus an *A* between the last *S* and the *Y* to make a strong point about grabbing life that way.

Writing all over my bathroom mirror means that my reflection is now splintered and smeared in a pretty murdery-looking red, but what the hell, this is what magic erasers are *for*.

In case you're wondering, what's actually going on here is that I have re-established contact with Saul. He emailed me on my birthday last week, but I ignored it, determined to lick my wounds properly until they formed a respectable crust, but now it's August, and I just found out through a mutual friend that he's moving to Calgary to stay with his parents and save money for a ticket to South America. I decided to email him and say farewell, good luck, thanks for all the fish. I intended to leave it at that, but then he wrote back, and then I wrote back.

I am not the newly stabilized person I have presented myself as in these emails to Saul, where I have written things like:

> You were also right, so right, about the timing. In hindsight, the timing was hilariously bad — if we had continued, it would have been a catastrophe. I was on an emotional trapeze. I was a complete fucking disaster. It frightens me in retrospect how unwell I was. So, there is some embarrassment. A lot of embarrassment. I've landed now. I've gained some footing, strength in solitude and all that.

Lies. All lies. But what was I supposed to say?

> Dear Saul, I am a bitter golem composed entirely of exhaustion and despair. I hate you passionately but I also want to marry you. I think about you when I

masturbate every single morning before falling asleep
with my pants around my ankles, listening to the dulcet
tones of Keith Morrison describing brutal femicides.

Recognizing that it probably wasn't a great idea to engage
with the person who was more concerned that I might accuse
him of poisoning me than with my actual well-being, I decided
to cut off contact last week. It's been six days since Saul's last
email, and in that time I have forgone my daytime sleeping
to go on two lunch dates: one with a fish-and-chip fry cook
who told me all the names of the seals at Fisherman's Wharf
(adorable), but whose teeth resembled rotting fence pickets; the
other with a self-described "executive" in his fifties who com-
plimented my enormous bum and asked to take me back to his
condo so he could see what it looked like bent over his kitchen
counter (I said no).

Anyway, do you know what Saul did after I stopped replying and blocked him on Facebook? He sent an email with the
subject line "Old-Fashioned Letter" and attached a photo of a
handwritten note:

Dear Elsie,
I am writing this letter to you in the journal you gave
me, weary pen in hand, with the hope of refining
my epistolary etiquette to aid in my world travels.
Perhaps it will contain the first whispers of my opus? I
kid, I kid, but already I have used it to put down notes
for my new novel, my sophomore work, which shall
focus on themes of alienation from Western culture,
travel as a means of escaping complicated feelings,
and reclaiming masculinity.

I wonder, was the journal meant to be a birthday gift, or a goodbye gift? I reconcile myself to the fact that it may be a goodbye gift, by virtue of you having unfriended me on Facebook (or did you block me? Maybe you just deactivated your account). Regardless, I wish to extend a hearty and heartfelt THANK YOU.

I am currently reposed in a hammock outside the cabin my grandfather built, where I am staying for a few weeks before I fly away to Colombia, where I shall teach English by day, feast on empanadas and *mujer hermosa* by night, and write like a fiend.

Tonight I am going hunting with my cousin. He hunts, plays the stand-up bass, and reads Foucault for fun! I should try to set you up with him. He's handsome and mysterious — women like that, right? He dragged me out and tried to set me up with a lady a few years back, but it turned out the lady in question was in love with him, and it was all a ploy to get her off his back.

I do hope you're well.

Best,

-Saul

All this called for was a polite thank you. In fact, it called for nothing at all, but of course I couldn't do *nothing*. Of course I couldn't. I had to print the JPEG and read it two hundred times and agonize over how to respond, which I eventually decided to do in kind, with a handwritten letter of my own, also photographed and attached to an email:

Dear Saul,

Thank you for the old-fashioned letter. I've been told that my handwriting is illegible. I don't agree, but if it is, I hope you're able to decipher this.

Much as I love a stand-up-bass-playing, Foucault-enjoying huntsman, I would not wish for your cousin to experience the same thing you did when he attempted to set you up and you realized the lady in question had someone else in mind. *wink emoji*

I'm excited for you, for your travels. Colombia, how exciting! I'm so happy you like the journal. It was a birthday gift, yes, but it became a parting gift. I think there's something special about handwritten things, and notebooks as vessels and companions for your thoughts. When you write something down on paper, it seems to be etched into your psyche somewhere. I can remember lots of the entries and sketches from my travels, though I haven't seen them in many years, since my mother's husband sent every treasure from my youth in her basement to the city dump immediately after she died.

You noted my absence from Facebook. Sometimes digital reminders can make missing someone worse, when you'd think it should be the opposite. Imagination, like social media, can be a gift or a terrible burden. For me, lately, both have been burdensome. I don't know what else to say.

You have my heart,

-Elsie

Yes, I actually handwrote "*wink emoji*."

I hate myself.

○

This whole thing with Saul reminds me of when I was seventeen and infatuated with this boy who had hair down to his waist that he wore in a long ponytail. He was tall and big with dazzling brown eyes that shouted *We are handsome and good at seeing the best moves in chess!* One day he called and invited me over to his house.

"Would you come by and brush my hair out for me?"

His hair was getting dreadlocks, he said, and he didn't want to look like so much of a hippie.

It was a Saturday morning when I got the call, and I was supposed to be helping my grandmother clean out her pantry, but I cancelled and drove over to his house with my heart burning in my throat. I was shaking when I knocked on the door, absolutely terrified and thrilled at the idea of spending time alone with him, of getting to touch his hair. *This is an honour,* I told myself, *and a day that you must brand into your memory forever.*

I thought it might mean he was in love with me. Why else would a boy invite a girl over to brush the tangles from his hair? Asking someone to brush your hair means something, something big.

Would he insist I get in the shower with him? Would he give me fragrant oils and make me wash his feet first and sing "Everything's Alright" from *Jesus Christ Superstar*? And while I was washing his feet, would he look down and realize that I was his soulmate, that I was born to wash his feet and kiss his knees and brush his hair forever? Would he be overcome with passion and pull me up to meet face to face, the water dripping off our noses? And would he grab my naked bum with one hand and the back of my neck with the other and kiss me with the power and glory of a zillion burning stars and then seed me with a glorious teenage pregnancy?

I was fully on board if that was what he had planned.

It looked promising when he opened the door in a Canucks housecoat, but then I noticed his hair was already wet. He'd just showered. I tried not to look as disappointed as I was when he handed me a bristle brush and a bottle of Pears conditioner and suggested we go down to the rec room and watch *Bill & Ted's Excellent Adventure*. On his couch, I sat with him on the floor in front of me, his head between my knees. It took the length of the movie to get his hair untangled, and when it was done, I kept combing for an extra ten minutes, not ready to give the moment up, trying to soak in the smell of his scalp. *Never forget this moment*, I told myself again.

"Pardon?" he asked.

"What? I didn't say anything."

"I heard you say something. 'This moment'?"

"Oh, I said we're done. This moment! All done now, ha!"

"Oh, great. Thanks, Elsie."

"You're welcome."

"I have some friends coming over to play *Tomb Raider* in a bit. They should be about half an hour."

I asked if I should go.

"Yeah," he said, "probably. Unless you want to play video games."

I don't like video games.

A few weeks after I combed the tangles out of the boy's hair, I hosted a Halloween party. My mom was a cool mom — she would stay upstairs and let her house fill up with rowdy teenagers.

I dressed as a forest nymph: covered myself in green glitter, glued leaves all over my body. The boy with the long hair dressed as a vampire, and he showed up with it slicked back in a long, smooth ponytail, which I admired as evidence of meaningful true love.

At the end of the night, I found out he was in the basement getting a blow job from my friend who was dressed as a sexy Dorothy from *The Wizard of Oz*.

I told Sam this story at one point, the whole story, including the blow job part.

"That's hilarious," he said.

"It's not hilarious. It's fucked up. Like, why would he ask me to brush his hair? What was the meaning in that?"

"There is no meaning."

"There is. And it is not hilarious."

"Okay, darling," he said. "Not hilarious. But teenage boys are just idiots. There's no more meaning to it than that. He just wanted the knots out of his hair."

"There was meaning. You don't know. Asking someone to brush your hair is meaningful."

We were lying in bed together, the baby sleeping between us. He stroked my face, my hair.

"Can I say something? Without you getting mad?"

"Yeah."

"I think it's time you let this one go."

I wish I could just let things go, but I can't. I just can't.

FIFTEEN

I got the coroner's report this morning. It took ten months for them to write three lines of text: *Cause of death: drug poisoning. Toxicology report demonstrated cocaethylene in addition to unambiguous markers of opioid use.*

I am trying to process this. I knew Sam was an alcoholic within a month of us moving in together, when I discovered bottles of hard liquor on the top shelf of the utility room cupboard, hidden behind the laundry soap.

I read it at least a hundred times — *drug poisoning, unambiguous markers of opioid use* — as if it might say something different if I just keep rereading. And what the fuck is "cocaethylene"?

I consult Dr. Internet and learn that cocaethylene is formed in the liver when it metabolizes cocaine and alcohol together. It's a cardiotoxin, a heart killer. It builds up in the bloodstream and causes intense euphoria, more than either coke or booze by themselves. Unfortunately, it also increases the risk of immediate death eighteen- to twenty-five-fold over cocaine use alone.

Why was Sam using cocaine? When was he using it? And what's this about "opioids"? Did he get some coke that was contaminated with fentanyl, or was he using heroin or oxy or morphine, too? How could I have missed this? Why didn't he trust me enough to tell me?

O

I know I should feel shocked and enraged and betrayed, but I've already been to the bottom of all those things. All I feel now is sorrow, exhausted sorrow. I consider the last six months of Sam's life. There was the night he got a phone call in the middle of dinner and was clearly pretending it was a wrong number, but then they called back twice. And that same night at 10:00 p.m., he announced that he was hungry again, that he absolutely needed to go to Burger King for a Whopper, it could not wait.

"Can't you just have more dinner? There are leftovers in the fridge."

"No, I need a Whopper. It has to be a Whopper. Only a Whopper will do!"

When he got home, I asked if he was having an affair. He laughed.

"A twenty-minute-long tryst on a Wednesday night? I like that you're jealous, but you're jealous of a hamburger. I just got a Whopper. See, here's the receipt."

"Why did you keep the receipt? You never keep receipts."

"I just happened to put this one in my pocket, I guess."

"Huh. Weird."

O

Because the universe likes to take dumps on my face, I also got an email this morning from my uncle. Ada May had a second limb amputated last night. If her circulation is that poor, why not just give her some extra sleepy-time chewies and let her drift away to Jesus?

She is so profoundly impaired at this point that she doesn't know who, where, or what she is. If you were to ask her this question: *Ada May, are you human, plant, or chair?* she would stare at the air for five minutes and then answer, "I dunno, Marge."

Because she doesn't know — she really doesn't. According to updates from my uncle, for the last six months, the only thing she has known is that there are people and things named Marge. That's the only word she remembers now: Marge. Nurses are Marge, doctors are Marge. Her dog is Marge, her lunch is Marge, my aunts and my uncles are Marges. I would be Marge, too, if I visited, which I intend to as soon as I get back to feeling like myself.

If you ask her what her name is, she will tell you she is Marge, though of course she isn't and never was.

Who is Ada May now? She is nobody. She exists somewhere between life and death, and any bubbles of earthly awareness that remain float up and pop on the hospital ceiling, while a confusing parade of Marges show up to interrogate the body below, change its catheter bag, shout in its face, *Do you know who I am, do you know why you're here, do you know, Ada May, do you know?*

At a family barbecue last summer, I asked one of my uncles if he felt sad when his mother called him Marge. He seemed offended.

"Of course I do!"

How would I know that he didn't want his mother forgetting who he was and calling him Marge? How could anyone ever know whether a person would like that or not? I would love it if an ancient, demented amputee version of my mother came back to life and called me Marge. *Yes*, I would say, *I am Marge. Just another Marge in a sea of Marges. And this Marge loves you.*

O

All of this news, the cocaethylene and opiates and the amputated grandma, is making me feel a little unhinged, which may also be related to the fact that I stopped taking my antidepressants cold turkey when my prescription ran out a few days ago. The first day was fine. My mood changed, but it was just a slight shift, the perfect amount of a shift. I could cry without wanting to jump off a bridge, I could laugh genuinely, I could listen to music and everything sounded fuller, deeper. My cells opened up. I sensed all the colours of songs. *This is nice*, I told myself. *You should always be this way. What are you thinking, numbing yourself with those pills? Fuck 'em!*

Day two was a little bit worse, but not intolerable. There were the brain zaps and the jitters, but it felt good not to be numb. *See, you just smiled at someone genuinely. Isn't that better? Fuck the pills!*

When I woke up this morning, I'd forgotten that I ever took pills at all. It had slipped wholly out of my awareness. But then. *Then.* Then the cocaethylene and opioid and Ada May news blew into my life, and the lack of medication came at me like a freight train loaded with barrels of self-loathing and tears, and it was too late. I'd fucked up. I was going to get hit, and there was going to be some kind of explosion on impact.

I held it together for a few hours — busied myself watering the garden (which is actually just a pair of carrots growing in a pot on the back porch), then did chalk drawings on the patio with Benji and Lark. In the afternoon, they both went to my sister's place for a sleepover. Now I am using my kid-free time to clean my kitchen, trying not to think about Sam buying drugs from some sketchy dealer or about the surgeon licking his chops when he sliced off Ada May's leg.

I am a very clean person, I say to myself as I stare at the sink, which contains a sideways casserole dish full of mouldy Kraft Dinner.

I put on Leonard Cohen's "I'm Your Man" and sweep the kitchen floor. Put it on again and reorganize the cutlery drawer. Again for the oven, again for the scrubbing of the cabinets, again for the pantry shelves, again for the fucking mother-fucking emptying of that cunt of a dishwasher with a cunt and a cunt and a CUNT YOU, you CUNT!

I smash a plate in the sink. On purpose. With all my might.

Look at you, says my reflection in the microwave. *Unhinged again, smashing your dinnerware. This is the reason you need your pills. You can't be a normal person without them anymore.*

"No!"

I manage to calm myself down by going to the store and buying some cigarettes. Smoking four in quick succession seems to do the trick. I am looking at a snarky celebrity gossip website and trying not to think about Sam taking me to that Leonard Cohen concert and squeezing my leg with his big, warm hand when the music swelled, and how our hearts swelled in unison.

I feel my heart rate slow and steady itself as I read about Claire Danes's fatal error in judgment at the Met Gala.

I don't know why this shit improves my mood so effectively, but it's better than box breathing or cold showers. Case in point: I am now composed enough to sit down to write a thoughtful response to my uncle's email about Ada May's amputation:

> If Grandma gets the other leg amputated, maybe someone can put a handle over her belly button so she can be picked up like a suitcase.
> Love,
> -Marge (Elsie Jane)
>
> P.S. Everything is going very well for me, thank you for asking.

Anyway, who's going to clean up these shards of shattered plate?

The last time I smashed a thing in the sink was right after my father died, almost two years ago now. It was a teapot, and I smashed it while I was in the middle of making dinner. I'd forgotten how many bay leaves I needed to add to the soup, and I had been in the habit of calling my dad whenever I needed cooking tips. When I remembered there was no more Dad to call, and that I would have to use the internet for all my cooking questions, I became enraged and the teapot had to die.

My dad was the person I could always call if I was feeling unhinged, the one person in my life that I could be a complete asshole around and he would just love me. If my dad was still alive, I would call him right now, and he would say, *Babe, it's just a plate; don't be so hard on yourself.* He would read me a passage from *The Four Agreements*, he would take me out to lunch at Ho Tong for the Szechuan shrimp special, and then we would go for a walk to the lighthouse at Ogden Point and he'd tell the same stories he always told me on our walks there. How he'd watched a fisherman get an octopus stuck to his face when he was seven. How he'd sneak under the docks and smoke cigarettes as a teenager. How he'd proposed to my mother there, at the lighthouse, and how her hair was black and glossy in the moonlight. He would tease me about smashing things, chuckle at my temper, call it passion and not insanity. He would compare me to my mother, whom he never stopped loving, even after she dumped him for the crime of getting depressed and lying on a foam mattress in his home office for two years.

I played Donovan's "Starfish on the Toast" for him on his deathbed. It was a song he'd been asking me to figure out on my guitar for ten years, and I couldn't be bothered to learn it until the day he died, sitting in a darkened counsellor's office at the Victoria Hospice, plucking along to a YouTube video. It was Thanksgiving night. All the other families in the world were gathered around crispy birds and mashed potatoes, wearing paper crowns, telling stories over pumpkin pies and coffee. My siblings and I were gathered around our dying father, whose body had been consumed, during my pregnancy with Benji, by a wildfire of cancer that began as a lentil-sized lump in his cheek.

Dad was on percussion with his rhythmic death rattle, and on the song's final note, he exhaled his last.

"Elsie, he's gone," my sister whispered.

We called the nurse.

My little brother was the first to let his sob out of the gate, and then we all crumbled. We huddled like penguins, kissed the tears off each other's faces. Sam was there, standing in the corner of the room, holding Benji and looking shell-shocked.

I got home that night and guzzled a whole bottle of wine. That's what you do after you watch your father die — you pump all the milk out of your tits and guzzle wine and blast "Starfish on the Toast" on repeat, filling your veins with blood-red booze until your brain throbs hard against its bone cage and you bob and swirl around the whole of the world's oceans all night long.

For the first few weeks after my dad's death, Sam spent a lot of energy trying to comfort me.

"Talk to me, Elsie," he'd say, and I'd stiffen, shake my head. "I don't want to talk. I don't feel like explaining things."

"Here, come here. Stop being so cold with me. Lean against me, please. Listen, you don't have to explain things. I was there. I want you to lean on me. I want to try to understand."

"Well, I don't want you to try to understand. I want you to accept that you don't understand and let me do what I'm doing, okay?"

A few times he took my face in his hands out of frustration, tried to twist his eyes into mine like screws. I smiled limply, squirmed away.

I didn't want to be reached, or seen, or comforted by anyone except my parents, and since that was impossible, all I wanted was to be a miserable turtle in my shell. Why couldn't he just let me?

"Nobody who's never lost a parent can understand what it's like to lose a parent, so you're not going to understand."

"I lost my grandma. I know it's not the same, but I loved her, and she helped raise me."

"Oh yeah, your grandma — wasn't she like eighty?"

"She was sixty-seven."

"You're right, it's not the same at all."

Eventually, after weeks of trying to connect and comfort and understand, Sam gave up. He began to treat me like a glass balloon, a depressing and delicate ornament that didn't make any sense and had no place in our home. He avoided and tiptoed around me. He got drunk and moped and stared at me from the other side of the room, hoping his hurt would draw me in. It didn't work. I pushed Sam away. I was haunted, untouchable.

At the time, I was sure that I would never recover from the loss of both my parents.

If only I'd known.

O

From: Sam <QBit_Sam@vergemail.com>

Date: September 29, 2011 at 1:08 a.m.

Subject: Re: Take a listen

To: Elsie J. <Elsiejane@vergemail.com>

It's become our song, hasn't it? "Calgary." Funny, it's not a romantic city.

It's our song, and yet it makes me sad. I can't quite put my finger on why. It's just a feeling that comes over me, a sadness about the death of love that coincides with the death of the body. How we know it's coming for us all, one day, and we love each other anyway. And in loving each other, we risk the kind of loneliness and abandonment that is much worse than it would be, had we never loved.

If we were forced apart by death or distance, I would hungrily paw at the floor for you. I'd pace, and obsess. As hungrily as then, as when we met last year, and as obsessed.

Sometimes I worry that you'll grow tired of me. Think me too old, maybe, and look for someone else to awaken and excite you in new ways. And then I run down that road, imagining if you left with them, and sailed away. I'd be on the shore, waving. I'd just stand there for years. Yeah, I think about that, sometimes. I wonder if I'd find my way back to life, or if I'd never leave that shore.

It's not that I feel insecure in this love, it's just that I'm prone to bad dreams, even when I'm awake. When those thoughts intrude, I remind myself that they're just as frightening as dreams of your house burning down, but no more real. No more real than any bad dream.

G'night, Elsie Jane.

-Sam

SIXTEEN

I HAVE COME TO CALGARY TO SEE SAM'S FAMILY AND celebrate his first empty birthday. Somehow autumn has arrived. The entire summer was a blur of heat and wildfire smoke; I remember almost nothing. Now the leaves are blushing orange and red and popping off their branches to frolic in the streets. There are pumpkin patches and honky geese and couples everywhere, walking arm in arm, enjoying kisses in coffee shops and meaningful looks exchanged between shelves at the library.

I woke up this morning with Benji's foot pressed into my face. He was sleeping horizontally, his tiny body somehow taking up the space of a whole man. I tried sneaking out of bed and into the bathroom for a shower, but he stirred and reached for me.

"Boobies," he murmured.

Lark stayed back in Victoria. I offered to bring her, but she didn't want to come and celebrate her dead step-parent's birthday, for some reason.

Benji and I missed our original flight yesterday because he ate about forty pieces of strawberry gum while I was packing and then puked it up on the way to the airport. I didn't realize what he'd done until the car filled with an ungodly bile-and-simulated-strawberry scent, and when I looked in the rear-view mirror, I saw that he had somehow silently vomited all over himself. He grinned at me.

"Did you eat Mama's gum?"

"No."

We had twenty minutes to make it to check-in before the cut-off. I pulled to the side of the road, unbuckled him, and pulled off his shirt as carefully as possible.

"Did you eat Mama's gum?"

"No, didn't."

We made it to the airport. I did not speed. I wanted to, but per usual I envisioned horrific accidents, so I kept it under the limit, parked in long-term parking, put Benji in the stroller, and ran like hell to Departures.

"Sorry, ma'am. Cut-off was five minutes ago."

"Five minutes? Please, I'm travelling alone with a toddler. I'm late because he puked in the car and we had to pull over."

The clerk was disgusted. "You shouldn't be travelling with him if he is ill."

"He's not ill — he ate a bunch of strawberry gum, okay? I'm sorry, but please. Please. It's my dead spouse's birthday and I'm going to Calgary to be with his family. I really don't want to wait until the next flight."

"Sorry, ma'am. Unfortunately, we can't accommodate you. The next flight is at five-thirty."

"That's in two hours."

"Correct."

"That's not enough time for me to go home and come back. Please, can you just squeeze us in? I promise I'm not trying to be a pain in the ass."

"This isn't my call. It's policy."

"Okay. I understand."

We somehow survived the two-hour wait and got through security without incident. (I had the Death Star cookie jar full of Sam in my luggage, and luckily they didn't bat an eye.) But once we got on the plane, Benji refused to sit down in his seat. The flight attendant cooed at him sweetly, gave him a toy airplane, offered him a package of cookies. He wouldn't budge. He stood on his seat, bouncing and making the most painful high-pitched squealing sound that has ever been made.

"Look, Mom," the flight attendant said, "we were supposed to take off ten minutes ago. I'm sorry, but due to safety regulations, we cannot start the flight until everyone is seated and buckled up."

"Can't I just hold him on my lap?"

"He's over twenty-four months, so unfortunately, no."

"Get off the flight, lady," yelled an old man somewhere behind us.

My eyes burned. The tears were coming.

I took Benji's hands in mine. "Look at Mama."

He stopped squealing and looked.

"I have to tell you something important, okay? It's a secret."

"Okay ..."

I leaned in and whispered in his ear, "Please, please, for the love of God, sit down in your seat. Please, Benji. I'll give you absolutely anything you want for the rest of your life."

He looked at me. Saw my tears. "Don't cry, Mama."

"Will you sit down?"

"No, I not sit down."

The flight attendant returned and pulled an extra-large Kit Kat bar from her pouch.

"You want this, my little friend?" She dangled it over Benji's head, and he tried to grab at it like a cat.

"Okay, but we have to be safe, okay? So you get to have this yummy chocolate bar, but first you need to sit down, put your bum on the seat, and let Mummy buckle you up so we can be safe and go for an airplane ride, okay, bud?"

"Okay."

He sat down. I buckled him. The cabin cheered and clapped.

By the time we were in the air, he was covered in chocolate. His hands, his face, his neck, his hair. But I was grateful. So, so grateful. And, in equal measure, angry. So, so angry at Sam for making me have to travel alone with Benji to celebrate an empty fucking birthday in the fucking first place.

I spent the entire flight seething, wishing I could grab Sam by the back of the head and shove his face in the mess he'd left.

○

Tonight, we're eating open-faced sandwiches with Danish stinky cheese. Sam's sister, Ingrid, has made a shrine: the Death Star cookie jar surrounded with candles on the buffet and an elaborate photo collage on the wall. Sam at age four when his bottom lip was stung by a bee, looking so like Benji. At age ten, dressed as a mummy for Halloween, and age fifteen, a handsome young nerd in an '80s wool sweater.

After dinner, we all dance to T. Rex, Nick Cave, Tom Waits, Leonard Cohen — all Sam's favourites. His dad, Magnus, swings Benji up in the air and onto his shoulders, and from behind, the shape of his body is so like Sam that I have an impulse to go and wrap myself around him and never let go.

There is birthday cake. Benji blows out the candles, but first we sing "Happy Birthday," which is ridiculous and sad.

"It *my* birthday?"

"It's your dad's birthday!"

"But where my dad?"

My heart is a rotting plum.

O

After the saddest birthday party ever, I lie down with Benji until he falls asleep.

I can't do my regular routine of pacing and smoking and fighting with ghosts here, as it would likely scare Sam's parents, but I can't sleep, either, so I tiptoe into the living room and look at the shelf that contains his old book collection. It's mostly sci-fi, but there are also textbooks on M-theory, artificial intelligence, machine learning, quantum physics. It's like running my fingers through his mind, flipping through this stuff; the part of him that lives in me wakes up and gets excited. If he had drained the pool, if he had emptied it even a little, he would have done so much with that beautiful brain. He had so much more to do.

I find a book I know: *I Am a Strange Loop* by Douglas Hofstadter. He wrote it after his wife died, and the book is him searching for meaning in the science of consciousness. Every individual exists as a particular point of view, Hofstadter says, and this perspective can also exist in other substrates, like in the brains of those who love us. We witness and absorb the subjective sensory patterns of those we love, just by virtue of spending time with them. And when they're gone, even when they're gone for good, a part of them stays within us. Our brains are love sponges, basically, soaking up the essences of our beloveds such that in their absence, we really can feel what they would be feeling, think what they would think.

I first read *Strange Loop* after my mom died, and it affected me so profoundly that I bought it again as a gift for Sam. I gave it to him at the airport when he was heading to Calgary on Christmas Eve in 2010, assuming he hadn't read it already (he had). On the inside cover, I'd written *For Sam. I'm so glad I met you.* We were still in that marshmallows-on-fire sweet burning of new love, then.

I am now back in bed. It's 2:30 a.m.

I feel like an imposter here, a leftover from Sam's life. Even as our son sleeps beside me, his chestnut hair wild on the pillow, a child so exquisitely beautiful it hurts, I feel like one of Sam's last poor choices.

What is left here for me?

I think of the dead woman behind SilverCity Cinema, how lucky she is to have found oblivion.

I think of Saul and his Scooby-Doo orgasms, how I laughed so genuinely every time. I wonder if I'll ever laugh again.

Do NOT email Saul, says my mother. *Have some self-respect.* But my laptop is already out, and my fingers are typing.

> From: Elsie J. <Elsiejane@vergemail.com>
>
> Date: November 8, 2016 at 2:52 a.m.
>
> Subject: I'm in Calgary
>
> To: Saul <saultyrivers@vergemail.com>
>
> Hi Saul,
>
> I'm in Calgary. I was celebrating Sam's birthday with

his family. I know you're planning on leaving for Colombia soon, but text me if you're still around and feel like meeting for a coffee.

-Elsie

I check my email as soon as I wake up and am delighted to find a new message from Saul.

From: Saul <saultyrivers@vergemail.com>
Date: November 8, 2016 at 8:22 a.m.
Subject: Re: I'm in Calgary
To: Elsie J. <Elsiejane@vergemail.com>

Hey Elsie,
I've changed my mind about Colombia. I've decided instead on Tahiti. Marlon Brando lived there, did you know that? I remember you mentioning that you loved A *Streetcar Named Desire*. Melville and Michener visited there too, and so many other greats. I'm back from my grandfather's cabin now. I'd love to hang out. The only thing is that I have three deer to butcher this morning. You don't want to see me with blood on my hands, do you? ;) I just noticed there's a show downtown I'd really like to see tonight. Would you come with me to the show instead of meeting for coffee?

-Saul

From: Elsie J. <Elsiejane@vergemail.com>
Date: November 8, 2016 at 11:14 a.m.
Subject: Re: I'm in Calgary
To: Saul <saultyrivers@vergemail.com>

Yes, good idea. Text me when you're done cutting
up animals!

I'm almost certainly setting myself up for another punch in the heart, but at the same time, the fact that *he* suggested meeting up at night instead of over coffee? It has to mean something. And is it so wrong to think that he's extending an olive branch to the possibility of a long-distance love affair across the Pacific, and that he might propose marriage upon his return? Is that so far-fetched? Not to mention that he went to all the trouble of emailing that handwritten letter last month. He's sending love signals. Yes, it's clear.

I spend the day preparing for the most romantic reconciliation in the history of morbid rebound relationships. I buy a new dress, a new scarf, black tights embroidered with poison ivy. I get my eyebrows waxed, shave my armpits for the first time in months. I primp and fret over eyeliner and blush and mascara in the mirror. And you know what? I actually feel almost normal. I'm not all puffy looking for a change, and my lips are so chapped from the dry prairie air that they have swollen to a sexy pout. I feel one thousand years younger.

"You look beautiful," says Sam's mom as I put my boots on. "You sure this guy is okay?"

"He's fine. I'll be fine. Don't worry."

There are tears in her eyes.

O

On the cab ride to the venue, I think of how tonight Saul
and I will laugh about the Clive's Classic Lounge/sidewalk
ambulance fiasco. *You're so stylish and poised tonight*, he'll
say. And *I'm so glad you didn't tell anyone I poisoned you!* We
will laugh and laugh, and then he'll take my face in his wild-
animal-butchering hands and absolutely murder it with kisses.
I've missed you, he'll say. *I need you.*

I walk into the venue with snow on my eyelashes and a song
in my heart. Saul is sitting in a booth at the back of the venue,
and I feel my guts sparkle and churn as I walk toward him in
romantic slow motion. There he is, in his sea-captain peacoat,
a thick knitted scarf around his neck and a blue toque pulled
low on his forehead, slumped against the crushed velvet of a
jumbo wingback chair. Looking a bit depressed, to be honest.

"Hi!" I say.

My every nerve is stretched to max capacity and vibrating.

"Hello," he says.

He doesn't get up to greet me, but it must be because he
is too overcome with emotion to be friendly to the person he
invited here.

"It's good to see you again!"

"Yeah."

I busy my hands by taking off my gloves and removing my
coat to reveal the new dress. He doesn't notice.

"So, here we are, both in Calgary!"

"Here we are," he says flatly.

The server arrives.

"Can I have a coffee, please?" I ask.

"Sure thing. Cream and sugar?"

"No, not a coffee. Actually, can I have a house white instead, please?"

"Wine?"

Wine.

"So, you must be excited about your travels. What's the itinerary?"

"Vaitape, in Bora Bora. Well, Vaitape *first.*" He sniffs.

"What happened to the plan for empanadas and *mujer hermosas?*"

"My friend Bianca's dad lives in Vaitape. He's letting me stay with him for free."

"Wow, that's awesome. I'm so stoked for you. You've wanted to travel for so long."

"Indeed."

Saul's coldness is upsetting. His slumping is upsetting. This whole thing is disorienting and not at all in keeping with my vision of the night. He's acting like a sullen teenager being forced to sit through dinner with a beautiful foreign exchange student while his mother talks about his childhood skin condition.

Within an hour, I am on my third jumbo glass of Chardonnay. Here's the thing: I'm not a drinker. No, really. I know you're wondering, because by now you understand that Sam was an alcoholic. But I've never been one to seek oblivion — not really; I consider myself more of a twice-a-decade, alarming binge drinker. On my thirtieth birthday I got absolutely trashed, and since then the only other time I've got *hammered* hammered was with Saul at Clive's. Which I'm not blaming him for — not at all — although I will note for the record that there is something about his attitude tonight, again, that is making complete and total oblivion seem attractive.

"I'm really sorry, again, about what happened back in June."

"Nothing to be ashamed of, I suppose."

"Oh, I'm *deeply* ashamed." I am trying to be cute and self-effacing, but he isn't into it. I need to work harder to lighten the mood.

"Yeah, that makes sense."

"Hey, remember that time you thought I was going to tell people that you poisoned me? Ha ha ha!"

"I'm glad you decided not to do that."

"Actually, I did tell everyone. Sorry. Ha!"

His eyes dart to mine for a millisecond. He manages an unconvincing smile, then goes back to peering limply at the stage from under his toque, both hands around his mug of beer like it's a sippy cup. God, he's beautiful, though.

I decide he might be interested in the dead woman behind SilverCity Cinema. I share with him the details of that coincidence and the last dream I had of her, which was just last night and featured her performing a *very* sexy dead-lady lap dance for Sam.

"So she was gyrating, like all seductively, but then her entire head fell off and landed on his lap and all these tiny birds, like the tiniest birds you've ever seen, like birds that had been shrunk by the *Honey, I Shrunk the Kids* shrinking machine, flew out from the top of her neck. Isn't that fucked?"

"Indeed."

He's giving me nothing.

The band starts sound check just as my face is flushing hot with embarrassment. Tears are coming. I excuse myself to the bathroom.

○

The third dead body I ever saw was another one from back in my mental health worker days. There was a client named Evelyn, and she needed a ride to the hospital to bid farewell to her spouse, Gerry, who had perished overnight due to complications from COPD. I was assigned the task, and though I'd never met her before, I felt fairly well equipped to support her through this journey, given my experience with the two other dead people, including my very own mother.

According to her chart, Evelyn had met Gerry when they were both housed at the same site five years earlier. After a year of sharing pizza and watching *Law & Order* together in the common room, they realized they were boon companions. They were married in the baseball field across from Tillicum Mall.

My colleagues did not warn me that Evelyn's legs were amputated above the knees, nor did they mention that she was the owner of the heaviest and creakiest and most cumbersome wheelchair in the universe. It's probably a good thing they didn't; I might have declined the task, which would have been my great loss.

Gerry had met his maker on the eighth floor of the Jubilee Hospital, a crisp and orderly unit for a crisp and orderly death. The nurses had the body washed and folded by the time we arrived. Evelyn wept and murmured to her dead love, stroked his fluffy, nicotine-stained beard for about an hour while I sat in a chair in the hallway to give her some privacy. I passed the time browsing discount wedding dresses online, though Sam hadn't proposed at that point and Benji was still a formless quark in our dreams.

On the drive back to her supported housing site, Evelyn cried softly and gazed out the window. We pulled into the parking lot. A pair of seagulls landed on my hood. Evelyn blew her nose into the rubber sleeve of her raincoat.

"You okay? Do you want a Kleenex? Here."

"I'm just so surprised he actually *beat* them."

"Sorry, beat who?"

"The tiny people."

"Oh, right."

"They've been keeping us locked in this dimension for over ten thousand years. I think Gerry must have caught one of them finally and tricked it into showing him the door back home."

"Oh wow. How does that feel to think about?"

"Well, it feels better knowing he got out of *here.*"

"That makes total sense. What did you love the most about him?"

"He stayed with me. And he battled the tiny people with me."

"He stayed with you and he helped you."

"He *believed* me."

She began to rock back and forth. Her eyes brimmed again with tears. Then she took a huge, gulping breath and shoved her whole fist into her mouth. When she finally exhaled, it was steam from a kettle, slow at first, then boiling to a howl.

"Evelyn, I'm sorry," I said. "I'm so, so sorry. For your loss, Evelyn. For your *loss.*"

O

Saul gives me a ride back to Sam's mom's place after the show.

"It was a good show," he says, suddenly relaxed and chipper.

"Yeah, it was good. They were good."

I am fighting the spins, which means I need to slide down in the seat, place my knees on the dashboard, roll down the window, and take sips of winter air.

"You okay?"

"Fine. I drank too much. Again, ha!"

He reaches over my legs to the glovebox and rifles around. "Hey, remember mixtapes? Did you ever make mixtapes for people you had a crush on?"

I groan. He picks a CD and slips it in at the red light. Leonard Cohen.

"Can you turn this off, please?"

"Why?"

"Never mind. Anyway, it must be nice to have absolutely no responsibility and be so free, hey?"

"It is. That's why I never wanted children."

"Oh, nice. Yeah, children are the worst. So, why don't you tell me all about all the magical fucking places you're going to see when you're travelling the world?"

"I'm actually thinking of going to the Middle East when I'm done with Bora Bora."

"Great. That's gonna be magical."

"It shall be magical indeed!"

"Oh, *indeed.*" Then I ask, "Hey, can I ask you a question?"

"Sure."

"Why did you invite me to the show tonight? Like, why did you even invite me?"

"What do you mean? I wanted to see the show. You suggested we meet for coffee, so I thought we could see the show instead."

"Pfft. *Right.*"

We pull up to the house. My heart is a prune, now hot and angry.

"I invited you to the show because I wanted to see you. I thought you said you wanted to be friends, and I care about you."

"You *care* about me."

"I do."

"Well, then, if we're friends, can you please just explain to me, friend, why you found it so fun to fucking fuck with my head so hard?"

"I don't th—"

"Like, fuck! Oh my God. Oh, good, I'm crying. Look, can we please just get out of the car and talk, and like actually fucking *talk*. Talk this through, resolve this, talk it out, whatever it's called?"

He turns off the ignition, shuts his eyes, and presses out a deep, arduous sigh. "Okay. Let's talk."

We stand on the sidewalk. It is 2:00 a.m., and he looks tired. Snow twirls around us, bright and whimsical.

"You invited me to the show and then you acted like a creep, like an asshole."

"I'm sorry. I didn't mean to."

"You didn't mean to *what*?"

"Hurt you."

"Well, you did. So much. So, so much." I start to sob.

"I would never want to hurt you. I didn't mean to. And it hurts me that you would think I would ever do that on purpose."

"You told me you were in love with me. On my back porch. And in my bed a whole bunch of times."

"I did say that. I thought I was."

"You *said* you were. Why?"

"I thought I was, at the time."

"No, you were toying with me."

"I wasn't. I'm not that person."

"You are that person to me. What's it like to be able to just drop feelings like garbage and drop human beings like garbage?"

He just stands there, dumb and terrified.

"Say something!"

"Elsie," he says, "I didn't fuck with you. I know I didn't because I'm incapable of telling a lie."

"What?"

"I couldn't have done anything to hurt you on purpose because I'm pathologically incapable of dishonesty."

I shake my head in amazement.

"*Fuck* you," I say.

I stumble into the house, hear his car door slam and his engine ignite. He's driving away.

Inside, I pick up the Death Star cookie jar and take it to the living room with me. I curl around it on the carpet like a mother cat. Hold it, rub it, kiss it, cry.

SEVENTEEN

THERE IS SO MUCH MORE TO LIFE THAN BEING WILD-ly in love. Having a soulmate really isn't all it's cracked up to be, actually. There's all the sex, for one thing, which is exhausting, because you have to kiss constantly. And when you kiss, you have to almost be eating each other like you're gobbling up the tastiest burger you've had in your lives. You also have to stare into each other's souls and use your eyes like ice cream scoops that both scoop out *and* deposit love through the rods and cones. After that, you have to nibble at and suck out bits of each other's vital essence by way of smooshing various body parts together. It's all very thrilling, but it can be gross, and it's definitely tiring. And once you get a bit too tired of it, once you start taking it for granted, other things start to creep in. Life things. Dysfunctional things. Addiction, finances, anxiety disorders, ADHD. Grief. That's when you go to couples counselling. Fortunately, couples counselling is a way to ensure that you and your soulmate end up sharing enchanted dances in the akashic space forever, even if you break up in this dimension.

Sam and I were going for regular therapy in the months before he died. We were seeing a lovely man named Jim, whose office was in the attic of a converted character house above the Salvation Army in a grubby part of town.

We talked to Jim about how we were fucking each other up — me with my seemingly bottomless grief over my dead parents (and the associated, anxious, constant fear that everyone around me was about to die, which, well …); Sam with his seemingly bottomless thirst for vodka (which he was back to attributing to work-related anxiety, "just a habit, not an addiction, a habit — understand the difference").

We also saw Jim separately, the idea being that we would work through our individual neuroses individually, our couple stuff as a couple.

I got back from Calgary last week and set to work sorting through Sam's old clothes, determined to follow his mother's instructions and stop hanging on to things. I found an appointment card for a session with Jim in one of his shirt pockets. The appointment was for December 9, 2015. Obviously, Sam had scheduled it unaware that he would go to sleep and die two days before he was supposed to be there.

On the back of the card were some words Jim had scribbled for Sam, ostensibly related to whatever they'd discussed in the last session: *Homework:* The Anxiety Workbook + Feeling Good *(David Burns).*

I felt bad that Jim had probably waited for Sam to show up on December 9, 2015. Jim had been pretty sad about that, I'd wager. He'd probably felt rejected and disrespected, so I decided it would be a nice idea to call and apologize on Sam's behalf for dying before his appointment.

That was my intention — a brief and courteous apology, an explanation — but when the call didn't go to voice mail and Jim picked up, I got freaked out and couldn't say the right words. I booked an appointment, as if things were normal, as if Sam was still alive and I was just getting back to thinking about counselling after a busy year.

"Jim here."

"Hi, Jim — this is Elsie. I saw you with my partner, Sam, last year?"

"Hi, Elsie. Yes, I remember you guys."

"Oh, good. So, but actually, I'm calling you right now because ... um. Because I'm hoping to book a session with you."

"Okay, sure. Let me take a look at my calendar."

"Great!"

"Elsie, I have this Tuesday at one or Wednesday at three. Or Friday morning. What works best for you?"

"Wednesday."

I hung up the phone and threw a pen across the room.

O

When I was a kid, the boy next door's name was Leo. He was a Jehovah's Witness, or his parents were, anyway. He hated going to Kingdom Hall on Friday nights, putting on that humiliating bow tie while the rest of the neighbourhood kids were playing capture the flag in our bathing suits. Off he would go with his weirdo parents, waving to us sadly from the back window of their car. Once, one of the neighbourhood boys threw a bag of milk at their car, and Leo's dad got out and grabbed the kid by the cuff of his coat and slapped his butt.

Another Friday, Leo hid in my garage while his parents searched the neighbourhood for him. I pretended he was a refugee prince and I was his kindly nurse. I brought him food, frozen dinner rolls that I microwaved until they were like hot balls of rubber, then presented to him in napkin-lined Tupperware.

We played together furiously, Leo and me. We were best buddies, building our forts deep in the forest and riding our bikes along desolate logging roads to the river, where we made oval sculptures out of clay, which we sold door to door, telling the neighbours how we'd come upon a trove of fossilized dinosaur eggs.

It was a wonderful friendship, until it wasn't. One day, Leo ruined everything by saying something very bad to me.

"I know a boy who likes you."

We were playing twenty-one in my driveway.

"No, you don't."

"I do. He told me."

"Who?"

Instead of just telling me who it was, he made me guess.

I went through the names of all the boys in the neighbourhood, bouncing the basketball, looking at the sky. Every name, every single name: I said them all.

"You're forgetting someone," he said.

"No, I'm not," I said. "I said everyone."

"You didn't say *everyone*."

It started to click. How he'd recently started tickling me all the time. How he'd been dunking my head underwater at the river, pushing me down at the park and sitting on my stomach so I couldn't breathe, spitting in my mouth. That these were acts of love suddenly seemed obvious.

I bounced the ball, looked everywhere but at him. I couldn't bring myself to meet his gaze.

"Are you going to guess again?" he asked.

I didn't know what to say, so I threw the ball as hard as I could at his face and ran inside.

O

All I wanted to do was say sorry to Jim, and to make sure he understood that we were not the type of people to no-show at appointments unless we were unexpectedly dead. Sam would have wanted me to do that because he really liked Jim.

I almost called back to cancel, but then I remembered how I'd stopped doing things like sleeping and showering. How I'd tried and failed to stop pacing my house and lecturing ghosts from 9:00 p.m. onward every night. Maybe seeing a counsellor who had known Sam and the terrain of our relationship wasn't a bad idea. Maybe Jim could provide some insight into what had gone wrong, where my blind spots had been.

Maybe he wouldn't be surprised at all that Sam was dead. Maybe Sam had told him all about using booze and drugs as anxiety-busters, and maybe that was why Jim had suggested reading some books instead. Maybe, but maybe not. How would I ever know if I didn't go see Jim again and ask him directly?

O

Do you know what happened to my neighbour Leo? I do.

After high school, he got a job selling electronics, worked his way into management. He married a girl from Texas, a Baptist, so he was excommunicated from Kingdom Hall and his parents would no longer speak with him. He bought a house in a brand-new suburb called Clovis Dream Heights, and one day his wife took their toddler son to the park. The boy went down the slide over and over, down the slide again and again. He went down the slide so many times that the mother lost count, as she would later tell the ambulance attendants when they arrived to attempt to revive the child. It could have been thirteen times or forty, it could have been fifty-seven times or ninety-three, before it was the last time, when he landed wrong and smacked exactly the wrong part of his head on the lip of the slide.

Does it matter how many times it happened, how many times he went down the slide and didn't die? Does it matter that she didn't count, that she didn't see death coming?

One thing I would like to make clear, by the way, is that I really liked Leo, too. I would like it to be known that when he was making me guess who liked me, I'd felt all hot and weird, and I was hoping it was him and trying not to hope, in case it wasn't. And I would also like to say that I regret the fact that I threw the basketball at his face, and that I gave him a bloody nose, and that he was no longer allowed to play with me, and that I never played with him again after that day. I liked Leo. For the record, I like-liked him. Such are the mysterious ways of love.

Anyway, she couldn't have seen it coming, Leo's wife. Nobody would ever know that such a thing could happen to a boy on a slide.

It was impossible for her to know.

O

To my surprise and in spite of my anxiety, I find myself immensely relieved to see Jim.

He opens his office door, and I have the immediate urge to shrink myself, strip naked, and crawl up to his chest, cling to him upside down like a newborn bat, his cashmere sweater lulling me into soft, deathless dreams. Jim could pet me, and then he could say, *Hoo now, hey there, little bat, there was nothing you could have done to save Sam.*

I would pay double his hourly rate for the baby-bat special.

Sensing that I need something, but not intuiting that it is to be a tiny bat, Jim offers me water. I say yes, and as he fills the mug, he draws close enough for me to smell him. Old Spice, plus some kind of Russian-y man perfume. Nothing like Sam.

I wonder if Jim's wife ever buries her nose in his armpits for five or ten minutes at a time, like I did to Sam, who never wore deodorant but always smelled of freshly turned earth and sex and salt licorice.

I sip the water, put a decorative pillow over my lap while Jim fiddles around in his desk, looking for a pen.

"Sam died," I say.

He doesn't hear me. "Lousy weather we're having these days, eh? Rain is endless."

Jim finds his pencil, saunters his cashmere over to the counselling chair, sits with one leg crossed over the other, and leans back. He has his little notebook and his mug of tea, and he's not expecting anything other than a regular old normal session of counselling yet another overindulged middle-class asshole. Then his eyes finally settle on me, really see me, and his face falls.

My entire body is puffy.

I look like I've been attacked by a vacuum that sucks out joie de vivre. Like I've been cut up and sewn back together all wrong.

"You're looking very uncomfortable, Elsie."

I attempt to deflect. "I've never seen you sit with your legs crossed like that."

"Oh? I do cross them from time to time, to the consternation of my wife and my chiropractor. You also haven't been here that much. What did we have, four or five sessions? Not enough to know my leg-crossing habits completely!"

He chuckles. A lighthearted chuckle.

"I can't cross my legs because they're too fat," I say.

The joke falls flat on Jim. His smile disappears and he raises his brows and closes his notebook, makes a point of uncrossing his legs. Then he leans forward with his elbows on his knees, hammering at me with his eyes like he's some tough-love high-school basketball coach about to give me a speech on the topics of self-respect and a winner's attitude.

"It's a pleasure to see you again, Elsie," he says.

"You too, Jim, and I'm super happy to be here again for counselling."

Jim has a bald head, a shiny one, with deep wrinkles in his brow from all the professional furrowing. His eyes have a softness I remember telling Sam I liked.

"He reminds me of a wise tortoise," I said after one session, "or a kindly cartoon penis with arms and legs. He's nice." Sam agreed.

Jim opens the notebook and scribbles something.

I look at the wall art: swans in some water; nondescript flowers in a vase; Einstein, the close-up of his face where his age spots look like constellations; a print of Klimt's *The Kiss*.

Sam and I had a print of *The Kiss* displayed prominently in our kitchen. I tore it down after he died and threw it in the recycling.

"Why do you have *The Kiss* in here?"

"Sorry?"

"Why would you put *The Kiss* in with a bunch of garbagey HomeSense art and a picture of Einstein?"

Jim looks at the wall, baffled.

"Sorry, which one is that? My wife decorated here. She's the interior designer of the two of us."

"It's the one of the man and woman kissing. *The Kiss*. That one right there."

It turns out that Jim doesn't even know it's called *The Kiss*. He never looks at the walls, he tells me, because he's too busy looking at the individuals seated across from him and concentrating on what they're saying.

"Well, just so you know, that's not an appropriate piece of art for this office."

"Why not?"

"Because it's a woman being kissed passionately by a very tall man. So for one thing it's pretty hetero and you probably have queer couples that come here, and for the other thing it's a bit rude to make people who are struggling in their relationships look at that. Like, what if it's some wife who hasn't been kissed properly in twenty-three years? She doesn't want to see that. Anyway, Sam is dead."

"D'you think it would make a difference if — Sorry, what?"

"Sam died. A year ago. Almost a year now, actually. He took drugs, and he died."

I watch Jim's sweet tortoise face absorb the news. He's clearly alarmed but trying very hard to be counsellor-ish and not betray any surprise or upset.

"I'm very sorry to hear that," he says. He does look very sorry. His tortoise face and tortoise mouth look sorry.

"It was an accident," I say.

Jim shakes his head in confusion. I see him trying to puzzle it all out, like why I wouldn't have mentioned anything when I called for the appointment.

I want to apologize, to explain to Jim how he fucked everything up by actually answering his phone, but it's too late now. He's looking and looking at me.

I stare at the Persian rug, dingy from thousands of unhappy-person shoes.

"You're looking very tired, Elsie. And no wonder."

I rub my eyes. "I am tired. Sorry. I'm tired."

I start to sob, and I sob and sob. And then I start to laugh, and I laugh and laugh.

"How are you sleeping?"

"Not sleeping. I don't sleep anymore — ha! I mean, what is sleep, some kind of alien?"

Again, Jim cannot catch a joke. He just stares at me, concerned as ever.

I smooth my skirt.

I sip some water.

"Have you considered getting something for that? For sleep? It can't be easy with the kids."

"No. Anyway, in case you were wondering, that's why Sam missed his appointment with you. It wasn't on purpose. He died. Surprise!"

"It is a surprise. An awful surprise."

"Is it?"

I spend the rest of the session trying to convince Jim to tell me if Sam had divulged that he was using drugs.

He won't budge, no matter what angle I hit it from. He's sorry, he says, but he can't discuss it.

"Even if it would help me sleep more than sleeping pills?"

"Even then. Sorry."

"But why can't you just tell me? How would you feel if your wife croaked after taking drugs you didn't even know she was using? I need to know. I have to know so I can understand what was going on. I have to understand to make sense of my life now. I have to, do you understand?"

"Let me ask you something," Jim says, "and this might be something you need to go home and think about, so don't feel like you need to answer me now. Here's what I want you to think about — are you ready?"

"Yeah, go ahead."

"Imagine I told you that yes, Sam told me he was using heroin and cocaine. He was using it every day, and he believed it was helping him cope with the stress of his life. You okay with this? It's just a hypothetical."

"Okay. Go on. I'm skeptical."

"That's fine, it makes sense to be skeptical. But okay, listen. Imagine that I told you it wasn't heroin or cocaine, it was skydiving. Sam was actually a skydiver, and he went skydiving every day to get out of his head and feel a particular biochemical sensation that he felt was helpful. Would you have been okay with him skydiving, even though it was a dangerous activity, if he was doing it not to hurt you, but because he felt like it helped him?"

"No."

"Why not?"

"Because jumping out of airplanes is a dumb thing to do."

"Why is it a dumb thing to do?"

"Because you can get hurt. Your parachute can fail, and you can smash into the ground. Everybody knows that. It's a disaster waiting to happen."

"Even if the statistics tell you that most of the time you jump out of the plane, your parachute will open and you'll be just fine?"

"Yes, of course! Fucking *yes*, Jim, because jumping out of airplanes is a ridiculous thing to do. Taking heroin and cocaine when you have young children is selfish and fucking irresponsible. So, no, I don't care how many times someone can do something and have it be okay, and I see what you're trying to do here, but I don't accept that line of thinking."

"Okay, Elsie. Well, look, we're clocking in at well over an hour here. Do you want to come back next week?"

"Maybe. If I do, I'd like to talk about my plan to jump dimensions so I can get the fuck out of this one. I need some advice about tying up loose ends."

"Your anger is so, so understandable. Here, have another drink of water before you go."

"I'm not angry, Jim. I'm just in love."

EIGHTEEN

ADA MAY IS DEAD.

She died a suitcase, as predicted. Actually, I think she might have had one arm and one leg left, one on either side of her body, so she probably looked more like a suitcase with one arm and one leg and an old-person head sticking out, but I can't be sure because I didn't see her.

I could have visited Ada May, but I didn't. I was too busy this whole year being sad about Sam and feeling sorry for myself after the disastrous reunion with Saul.

My sister was over for coffee when I got the phone call. It was my uncle George, Grandma's youngest child and the only one of my mother's siblings I had really stayed in touch with since her death.

"She was comfortable," George said. "She slipped away in the night."

"Thanks for calling," I said. "You okay?"

"I'm okay. It's not a surprise."

My sister's phone rang as soon as I hung up. Same uncle, same news.

I scrolled through my phone and found a pic of Ada May and me. It was from that barbecue on my uncle's patio, the one Sam had come to. I was kneeling beside her, my arm linked with hers.

I uploaded it to Facebook and posted a short and loving tribute: *Good night, Ada May. Sweet dreams.*

How graceful and inscrutable she was. She was born in Winnipeg, and met our Irish grandfather at a dance. They had five children together, moved to B.C. He built the Malahat Chalet, then opened the gift shop at the Empress Hotel. She was the charge nurse at the Victoria General Hospital. That's it. That's all I know. She never talked about her life, not to me. She didn't pass much of anything on, aside from a love of reading. I spent hundreds of hours with her, maybe thousands. Picking berries, helping her bake, going on long walks, working in the garden. Everything we did together, we did in loving silence.

"I loved picking blackberries with her," I said to my sister. "We would each fill up two ice cream buckets."

"She never did that with me."

"She took you on a cruise, though."

"That was only because Grandpa died and she had the extra ticket."

"Did you talk much on the cruise?"

"Not really. We both pretty much read the whole time."

"I wish I knew more. I wish I had asked more."

"She wouldn't have told you. She was a mystery. Anyway, I'm still mad at her for going to France when Mom was dying."

"Yeah, that was weird."

My phone rang again. It was Uncle George calling back.

"Hey, George."

"How *dare* you!"

"What?"

"I didn't get a chance to tell my own children that their grandmother died, and they *saw it on Facebook*? How goddamn insensitive can you be?"

"Sorry, what? I'm confused."

"I am furious. I'm fucking disgusted."

click

My sister's phone rang immediately. Same uncle, same rage — only this time he was raging to my sister about me, unaware that we were in the same room. I heard every word. *Fucking insensitive, selfish bitch.* My sister couldn't get a word in, but she didn't try to defend me. When the call ended, she looked shell-shocked.

"I heard that," I said. "Why didn't you stick up for me?"

"I couldn't get a word in edgewise."

"But everyone posts on Facebook when their grandparents die!"

"I know. If it hadn't been you, it would have been me. I was about to post something, too, right before he called."

"So why didn't you explain that?"

"I didn't get a chance to say anything."

"You were saying, 'I know, I know.' Who the fuck doesn't tell their own children about a dead grandma first? Who tells their nieces before their own children? How was I supposed to know that he hadn't told his own kids before he told me?"

"I just don't have the bandwidth for this right now. I'm exhausted."

She picked up her youngest child and instructed the older one to put on her coat.

"You're leaving?"

"I'm not feeling well."

"Why didn't you defend me? Why didn't you say *anything*?"

"His mother just died, Elsie. He doesn't know how to deal with being sad, so he's angry and lashing out. It sucks that you have to be the scapegoat — I'm sorry."

"I don't give a fuck that his mother just died. My mother died. My father died. My spouse died, and I didn't scream at anyone, and I had to be inundated with Facebook posts all day long from everyone who ever met Sam and tagged me and I didn't call to scream at them!"

"His mother *just* died."

"She was ninety-six!"

"It doesn't matter. She was his mother."

"I can't believe you didn't defend me."

I looked at my sister. She was exhausted from nursing a toddler and working full time to maintain the benefits that her older daughter with cystic fibrosis relied on to survive.

"Please don't go," I said. "I'm sorry. I'll stop crying and ranting."

"I'm too tired for this," she said. "It's too intense for me. I have to go home now."

"But what about *me*? I'm tired! *I'm* exhausted!"

She opened the door and ushered her children to the van. I followed her outside in my bare feet, still in my pyjamas, Benji on my hip. Starla was vacuuming out her truck.

"I can't believe you're being so cold to me and just leaving after this happened."

She closed her eyes, took a deep breath. "I know this might be hard for you to believe, but you're not the only person capable of experiencing grief."

"What? I *know* that! You don't think I know that!"

I couldn't believe it. I couldn't believe that *I* had been cast as the villain in Ada May's death. I imagined my uncle, his self-righteous phone call campaign to everyone else in the family, my other uncle and my aunts, my cousins, all of them agreeing that I was surely the most selfish and insensitive person alive.

"Nice, real nice, Rachel," I said. "Yeah, why don't you lecture me about grief, because I don't know much about it. Maybe you can get some rest in your beautiful renovated house with your alive husband there to help with the kids. Have a good rest, okay? Have a really great rest."

I seethed. I seethed and paced and sobbed and raged. About Uncle George, about Sam, about my sister who had absolutely no right to be exhausted with me. She had no right, no right at all.

Grief is an utterly selfish state of mind. Nobody can possibly understand the depth and complexity of your pain, the scale of your loss. It blinds you. It blinds you to so, so much.

O

When my daughter Lark was born, my mom was over the moon. It was her first grandchild, so she emailed everyone in the world.

From: Daphne <daffydaph_54@vergemail.com>
Date: May 29, 2006 at 4:37 a.m.
Subject: Over the MOON!!!!
To: <all contacts>

I am simply over the moon with the birth of my beautiful granddaughter! Her name is Lark Daphne (after

me!). She has all 10 fingers and toes and rosebud lips!
I'm over the moon, folks! Take a look at the 32 pictures
I've attached and don't hesitate to ask for more!
Love,
-Daphne

She was over the moon, but I was decidedly earthbound, startled and confused by this strange creature that seemed to have emerged fully formed and out of nowhere. I knew I'd been pregnant — I had been there for the positive tests, the ultrasounds, had stood naked in front of the bathroom mirror and with detached curiosity examined the rivulet stretch marks that wound up and down my middle, more and more of them as the weeks had rolled along. I also knew that I'd pushed something out of my crotch, because I'd been there for that, too. It was just that I couldn't recognize this baby as kin, this ferocious organism with her wolflike eyes and clenched fists and hungry mouth. Surely she hadn't come from me?

"Oh, she's yours, all right! Look at her face; she looks just like you did!"

I was so blitzed after labouring overnight that Mom stayed at the hospital and took care of all the meconium. Did you know about meconium? Because that is some weird shit. I'd read about how a baby's first poop was thicker, but this stuff, it was like my kid was a toothpaste tube full of tar. I just sat there astonished, my milkers hanging out of my hospital gown, watching Mom hold Lark's legs in the air. She was wiping and laughing away like she thought this endless tar coil was the cutest thing in the fucking world.

"Do you know what I did for the whole first month after you were born?" she asked, still catching the poop, wiping, chuckling.

"You stared at me."

"I just sat there in my chair, and I just took that little baby in my lap, and I just stared at her beautiful face."

"That's really sweet, Mom."

"… That baby was *you*."

"I know."

I thought I could escape the hospital with a modicum of dignity intact, but it was not to be. A big, mean nurse arrived and told me I had to demonstrate my understanding of the peri bottle. A peri bottle is something only birthing people know about. It's a special water bottle that you squirt on your perineum stitches to keep them clean.

I was unsteady on my feet, my thighs trembling, still dripping baby curds.

"I know how to do it. You just squirt," I said.

"I still need to see you do it before you can be discharged."

"But I'm not comfortable. I have a pad on, and it's full of stuff."

"It'll take thirty seconds, and then you can get ready to go."

Mom had swaddled the baby and was singing and bobbing her around. I waddled to the bathroom, followed by the nurse, who leaned against the door frame and looked grumpy. I pulled up my gown, pulled down my mesh postpartum underwear, and squatted over the toilet.

"Like this, right? See? Squirty-squirt-squirt."

"Good enough."

On the ride home from the hospital, I realized for the first time what a treacherous world I had been living in all my life. I might not have been overwhelmed with loving bubbles of oxytocin postpartum, but the adrenalin was pumping through me just fine. I was on high alert for all possible threats. They were everywhere. Cars: Dangerous. How many people behind the wheels of those things were serial killers and pedophiles and baby stealers? Telephone poles: Unbelievably dangerous. One unhappy guy with a chainsaw and we'd be crushed instantly.

When we arrived home, I refused to get out of the car until my husband moved the hose snaking across the driveway.

"I could trip on that and the baby could go flying."

"I'll carry the car seat, then."

"No, you could get hit by an asteroid."

He moved the hose. I tiptoed along the rock path like there was hot lava on either side of me. This was the hyper-vigilance that coloured my world after Lark was born, the same dread force that came rushing back into me when Sam died. I couldn't sleep, even when Lark slept; I was convinced that I was keeping her alive through the sheer force of my will, and if I took my eyes off her to eat or sleep, she could slip back into the void she had arrived from.

My mom, though: she was radiating calm and sweetness and warmth, as if intent on demonstrating how much more perfectly she could love my child than I could. The same infant who'd been tomato faced with rage would melt instantly into her arms and fall asleep.

"Do you know what I did when your mama was born, Larky bear? I just took that little baby — just like this — and I propped her up in my lap — just like *this* — with her little legs like *this*, and do you know what I did? I just took that little baby, and for a whole month I sat and stared at her beautiful face."

When Lark was four months old, my feelings for her began to move beyond the simple mammalian impulses to fight pred-ators and stuff her with milk. I fell in love, finally. I'm just not a person who falls in love right away, I guess. Maybe the reason it took a little longer was because I knew that my mom was dying from the time I got pregnant. I thought if I could somehow budget my love correctly, I could hang on to both of them.

Mom stopped chemo in early July, when Lark was six weeks old. By the end of that summer, the cancer had flooded her abdomen with ascites so that she looked like she was due to give birth any moment herself.

There are only a few times in life that adults get a pass to act like spoiled children. One of them is right after you've had a baby, and your mom is there, and you get to cry to her about how tired you are and how your tits are on fire and you're fat and you want soup. And she will mother you then, and she'll get you your soup, and she'll take that little baby and stare at her beautiful face and be over the moon.

When Mom was initially admitted to hospice, the doctor wouldn't discuss life expectancy. It was too difficult to predict, he said; every patient was unique. But then we had a family meeting, which was called to discuss the transition from hospice to home and to get clear on the logistics of mom's care needs. During the conference, Uncle George opined that he had tickets to France with his mother. He wanted to take Ada May to Provence, as he had every year since his father died.

"The château has already been paid for," he said.

"I don't think France would be high on my priority list right now," said my sister.

"It's booked," he snapped.

"Listen," the doctor said, "we know it can be a challenging time to make decisions when a loved one is palliative, especially around travel plans. So, if it's okay with you, Daphne, I'd like to share a bit about the conversation we had this morning, when we were discussing end-of-life."

My mother, gorked on morphine and haloperidol, sat serenely in her wheelchair, staring at a glittering red maple tree outside, her bald head covered in soft white fuzz.

"Daphne? Is it okay if I share?"

"Huh?"

"Is it okay if I share what we talked about this morning?"

"Oh. Sure."

She was completely engrossed in her study of the air and the leaves.

"Okay, folks. So, what Daphne and I talked about this morning was that it can be challenging to predict what exactly will happen in the course of this illness. However, there are a few things that can help us understand where we are in this process of palliation. One of those things we typically look for is a change in sleep-wake patterns, maybe even a little bit of confusion, which we've seen over the past few days."

A few nights earlier, hospice staff had found her up at 2:00 a.m., trying to give her roommate a sponge bath. She had been a nurse for thirty years, and she thought she was working on the unit. They thanked her for helping, guided her gently back to bed, and gave her an Ativan to lull her back to sleep.

"Another thing we start to see is that the person becomes less interested in food and water, and that's beginning to happen with Daphne."

I asked what he was actually saying. He put his chart down on the coffee table and clasped his hands.

"I'm saying that we're looking at weeks. Maybe a month. Maybe."

They went on their three-week vacation to France anyway, George and Ada May. We received email updates with pictures every few days: Ada May eating a baguette with brie under a pergola dripping with grapes; wearing a wide-brimmed hat and smiling in the autumn sun, fields of lavender and sunflowers rolling behind her; posing gracefully on the Pont d'Avignon and by the ocean in Saint-Tropez. Meanwhile, my sister and I were changing her daughter's diapers, moistening her lips with Vaseline, turning her over so she didn't get bedsores.

O

On the last day of my mother's life, she got a sudden burst of energy. I was sitting by her bed, breastfeeding Lark, when she sat up, looked at me, and announced, "I'm going for a run."

"You can't run now, Mom," I told her softly.

"Get me my shoes," she ordered.

"Mom, you can't run right now."

"I can't?"

"No, you can't."

"Why not?"

"Because it's just not running time. It's resting time."

"It is?"

"Yeah. Lie down. Here, I'll get your blankets back on."

"Don't want blankets."

"Okay, then just lie back without your blankets."

She closed her eyes and drifted off. Lark had fallen asleep at my breast, so I moved her to the cradle beside the hospital bed and crept out of the room to get a snack. I was eating a piece of toast in the kitchen when I heard her calling.

"Elsie Jane? Elsie? Elsie Jane? Elsie?"

I hurried back to her bedside. "You okay?"

"I just wanted to talk about the joke."

"What joke?

"Did you ever hear the one about the guy who took a five-year shit in the woods?"

"No, but that sounds funny."

"It is funny."

"What's the punchline?"

"He took a five-year shit in the woods."

We both laughed.

"I love you, Mama," I said.

"I love you, too," she said, closing her eyes. "I'm going to be a bear in the water now."

"Okay, you go be a bear in the water."

"I am."

NINETEEN

TWO NIGHTS AFTER ADA MAY DIES, AN OWL COMES. I WAKE UP
at 3:00 a.m. and am getting a glass of water when I see it perched
on the backyard fence. I put on my housecoat and go outside.

She lets me approach her, and when I'm an arm's length
away, she says, "Hoo."

"Grandma?"

"Hoo," she says again, blinking slowly.

"I'm sorry I didn't visit you," I say.

She puffs out her feathers, grooms the plumage on her rear
end, and flies off under the moonlight.

The next night, I set my alarm for 3:00 a.m. and go outside
to wait, sure Grandmother Owl will show up again. I stand
on the deck, smoking cigarettes, staring at the oak tree and
imagining its branches holding the tree house Sam wanted to
build there for the kids.

After about fifteen minutes with no sign of the owl, I sit
down on the patio steps. Maybe she isn't coming, or maybe I

was supposed to yell for her. I decide that must be it, so I take a big breath and holler, "Grandma!"

As soon as I say it, there is the unmistakable sound of owl wings flapping in the night. *Floosh, floosh.*

There she is, looking as regal and grandma-ish as any owl ever has.

"Hi. You came back."

"Hoo."

"I love you, Ada May," I say, "so much. Thank you for visiting me."

I love you, too, the owl says with her eyes.

There's a rustle in the grass. The owl bobs her head excitedly, opens her beak to hiss, and then, in a tornado of feathers, swoops into my yard. Her prey makes a horrific squealing sound.

She hops up right beside me on the patio. There is an obese rat in her left claw, velvety and twitching.

"Oh my *God*, Grandma."

She swivels her head and gazes at me dispassionately, blinks, and then daintily plunges her beak into the rat's belly and pulls out its guts while it's still panting.

○

When my mom advised me of her plan to be a bear in the water, I knew she would be leaving soon. Sometimes you just know things. I just knew.

"I have a feeling it's going to be tonight," I told my aunts, who had returned to the house to relieve me of my duties.

"It's not going to be tonight," said one of the aunts, who was a palliative care nurse in Nova Scotia. "She ate a bite of quiche this morning, and she asked for a sip of milk. If it was gonna be tonight, she wouldn't be eating or drinking at all. Take your baby home and get some rest."

"I can't. I just have a feeling. I have a feeling it's going to be tonight."

"Well, Grandma's in the air from Paris and she's not getting in until two a.m., so I hope it's not tonight."

I went home, ate dinner with my husband, and called my siblings.

"We need to be there," I told my sister. "She's leaving tonight."

By the time we made it back to her bedside, she was unconscious. Her breathing had become jagged and noisy, secretions gurgling in her throat.

"What's wrong with her breathing?" my brother asked an aunt.

"They're called Cheyne–Stokes respirations," she said. "She just had a breakthrough for pain, and she's comfortable, I promise. It sounds bad to us, but it doesn't bother her."

I lit votive candles, put on Joni Mitchell's *Blue*, soft in the background. We took turns sitting alone with her. She couldn't move or open her eyes, but when we said certain things, certain emotional things, she moaned.

At 1:30 a.m., I was so tired that I couldn't see straight. The Cheyne–Stokes respirations had gotten so loud they were rattling the walls. *Blue* was on its eighteenth rotation.

"I can't believe she's hanging on like this," my sister said as we took a break in the kitchen.

"I know," I said. "I think she's waiting for Grandma."

"I think so, too. Fuck."

"Did you say goodbye?"

"I did. I said it's okay to go. I said we'd be okay."

"Ha, that was a lie."

"Total lie."

"I told her the same one. Just let go, we're okay, and then she made that moaning noise."

"Yeah, she did the same thing with me. It was awful."

"I think I have to lie down. I'm so tired I feel like I'm going to die. Ha!"

"I'll come lie with you."

One of the aunts said she would wake us up if anything changed, so we went downstairs to the room where Lark was sleeping and crawled into bed together, drifted off to the rhythmic death gurgles filling the house.

We were woken up by our brother banging on the door.

"Get up. Grandma's going to be here in five minutes. They're on their way from the airport. Better come upstairs."

Back at the bedside, Mom was now positioned on her back, still making the horrible gargling noises.

When Ada May walked into the room, she did not look at all like a woman who had just spent three weeks touring the south of France. She had to be held upright by my two aunts. She was frail and frightened.

She went to her daughter, held her face in her hands, kissed her forehead.

"I'm here now, Daphne," she said. "I'm here."

And then my mother, who had been unable to speak since the day before, mustered the last of her strength to say, "Mama."

And that was it. She was gone, her mouth still forming the soft open "ah."

Ada May gripped the bed rail, about to collapse from grief. One of the aunts helped her over to a chair.

Who the fuck goes to France while their daughter is dying?

TWENTY

THE LAST SIX MONTHS OF SAM'S LIFE WERE A DEATH spiral. I can see that, now — hindsight 20/20 and all that. In the spring, my maternity leave ended, and I went back to work full-time. Me working coincided with a massive increase in his drinking. One or two glasses of wine became one or two bottles. By mid-May he was drinking wine or beer daily. I found empty mickeys of vodka under the seat of his car.

One night, he woke me from a deep sleep.

"What's up?" I asked.

"I need to smoke some pot!"

"What?"

"I want to smoke weed!"

"You don't even like weed. Are you drunk?"

"No, I had one beer two hours ago. I'm fine. But I'm going to go to Blair's and see if she has any weed, okay? I'll be back in a couple hours."

"What's the urgency? You don't even like weed."

"I don't know. I just really want some weed!"

Three hours later, he shook me awake again. "Hey, hey, get up! I got us some weed!"

"I hate weed. I was sleeping."

"Just come outside with me, then, while I have it."

I pulled myself out of bed, followed him upstairs. At the kitchen table, he pulled out a baggie.

"That is not weed."

"Yes, it is."

"Where did you get that?"

"Blair wasn't home, so I went to the bar on Cook Street and a guy sold me this."

I took the baggie, held it up to the light. There were a few small green chunks, and the rest looked like ground-up glitter.

"This has powder in it. What is this? I would throw it away if I were you. Don't smoke this, Sam."

The next morning, he wasn't in bed. I was nursing Benji on the couch when I heard the kitchen door slam.

"Hello?"

Sam came tumbling into the room like Kramer, his eyes bloodshot and wild, sweat pouring off his forehead.

"What the fuck is wrong with you?"

"They tried to break into the house last night," he said breathlessly.

"What?"

"They tried breaking into the house, but it's okay. Don't worry. I took a chair outside, and I got *this* chef's knife and I guarded the door in case they came back. And they did come back! They were whispering under the deck, and I chased them away and saw their shadows running like assholes."

"Put that knife down."

He put it down on the coffee table and started pacing and gesticulating, shaking his fists, mumbling.

"Wait, did you *actually* see someone try to break into the house?"

"No, but I heard them. I heard them whispering outside, talking about breaking in. I chased them away, and I saw their shadows running."

"There's something wrong with you. Did you smoke that stuff last night?"

"Yeah, but that has nothing to do with it. *Understand.* I heard the footsteps, I heard them whispering, and I saw the shadows running away. *Cowards.*"

"Oh my God, you're high. You're so, so high, Sam. How much of that stuff did you use?"

"Why won't you listen to me?"

"How much of that stuff did you use?"

"All of it, but that doesn't matter. *Listen*, I heard the guys talking about breaking in and taking you and Benji. *Kidnapping.* They had planned the whole thing, those fuckers."

O

I dropped the baby off at my sister's place and took Sam to the hospital.

Four hours in the waiting room, watching him pace around. He was given a urine drug screen: cocaine in his bloodstream.

"I thought it was just weed," he told the emergency room doctor.

"Where did you get this 'weed'?"

"From Logan's Pub. A guy sold it to me."

"Well, there's your first problem."

I shared that the baggie had appeared to contain glitter. The doctor bunched his lips and shook his head.

"I'm going to give you a medicine called labetalol for your blood pressure. It's sky high, and your heart is racing. I'm also giving you this. This is lorazepam. It'll help calm you down. You need to go home and go to sleep. And apologize to your wife, if you haven't already."

After that, I insisted that he make a doctor's appointment. He agreed that his drinking was out of control, that this latest fiasco was evidence of his anxiety being so acute that he needed medical intervention. We went to see his GP the next week. In the appointment, Sam cried. He admitted that he was an alcoholic.

The GP prescribed an antidepressant, plus lorazepam and Antabuse. Then, for reasons that remain an infuriating mystery, he insisted that *I* witness the daily dosages and keep the pills away from Sam.

"I don't feel like this is a good idea," I said. "I'm his partner, not his case manager."

"It'll work out fine. Right, Sam?"

"Sure thing."

It was not fine. He filled the prescriptions and hid the bottles immediately. He refused to let me "witness" anything. Two weeks after the appointment, I found the empty bottle of lorazepam in the bathroom trash can.

"I think you should go to proper treatment," I said. "Your parents would help. There are resources for you in your benefits to help cover the cost."

"I'm not fucking going to treatment, okay? Got it?"

"Okay, but what about a group? I bet you'd meet people you would end up liking and admiring. There are all kinds of people who go to AA."

"I told you, I'm not doing abstinence. Twelve-step groups are brainwashing cults. I've figured out a way to use the Antabuse to help me establish a safe pattern of drinking only on weekends."

"Well, drinking on weekends still means bingeing and ruining our family time. I don't think Antabuse is meant to be used that way, and Dr. Ribinsky said I was supposed to be holding onto and witnessing it."

"No. Let me be nice and sparkling clear, okay? Look at my mouth. *No*. I'm not a fucking child."

"Yeah, and I'm not a case manager. I don't want to fight with you; I want you to get help. This is ruining us. It's ruining our lives. The kids spent all morning and all afternoon waiting for you to get out of bed and take them swimming. You're breaking promises to them. Is this how you want them to remember their childhoods?"

"Leave me alone, okay? I like drinking. I *like* it. I'm not an alcoholic, I just like it. It got out of hand, I went to the doctor, and now I have a plan to adjust my behaviour using the Antabuse. I don't want to talk about it anymore, understood?"

"But you admitted you were an alcoholic at the doctor ..."

"I was just saying what I needed to say to get the benzos!"

"Wow. Have you even been taking the Antabuse? The antidepressant?"

"I've been taking the lorazepam and the Effexor, and I take the Antabuse on days when I don't want to drink."

"Sam, that's not how it works."

"Okay, *Doctor Elsie*, why don't you tell me in all your studied wisdom how it works?"

O

Tomorrow is the day. The deathiversary. I dreamed of him last night, of Sam. I was following him into the forest behind SilverCity Cinema, calling his name. When I finally caught up, I waved my hands in front of his face, pulled on his jacket sleeve.

"Sam? Sam! Look at me, *please*!"

I grabbed his hand.

He froze, stood stiffly, and stared straight ahead. And then, in a robot voice, he said, "Don't grab my hand. Why are you grabbing my hand? Don't touch me."

I let go, and he was back in motion. He veered off the trail and ducked into the bush, then parted the branches of a cedar tree like curtains and stepped into a clearing. A bed was there, our bed, but with another woman under the covers. *Her.* The dead woman again, this time dressed in a lace teddy. Her skin was still mottled, but her jaw was intact and her hair wasn't matted with death. It was styled just like mine, dark with wild waves. Sam went to her, crawled under the covers, nuzzled her neck. She stroked his beard, kissed his forehead.

"I love you, Sam," she said.

"I love you, too, darling," he replied tenderly, and then the ground opened like a mouth and swallowed both of them whole.

O

She's haunting me, the murdered woman, but it wasn't until this morning that I understood why. I didn't understand her significance, but now that I do, I can't get it out of my mind. I feel so foolish that it took me so long to clue in.

It's me. It was always me.

In the dreams, she has my face, but it's not just that. The newspaper articles: dark hair, midthirties, stretch marks, blue sweatpants. Even the scar on her abdomen — I have *that scar.* It's from when my doctor accidentally perforated my uterus with a copper IUD and I had to get it removed via laparoscopy. And I *love* those blue sweatpants.

The dead woman wasn't murdered. There is nothing suspicious about her death. Nothing suspicious, but something magical.

She was trying to jump through space-time and rescue Sam.

Somehow she made a wormhole and jumped through it, but her body couldn't handle the jump. She was asphyxiated in the wormhole, or maybe upon landing.

This changes fucking everything.

From: Sam <Qbit_Sam@vergemail.com>

Date: March 10, 2014 at 2:10 p.m.

Subject: Still a kid

To: Elsie J. <Elsiejane@vergemail.com>

I told you I wanted to be as sincere as possible with you. Here's something sincere, that I've been keeping to myself: I'm afraid to go back to school, for the Ph.D. I'm afraid that I may have nothing to contribute, after all. Like the fear of going to a party, perhaps, and finding that no one is interested in what you have to say. That all of your observations and comments are boring, obvious. It's a new fear of mine, at least in that I haven't known it since adolescence. I don't know what to do with it. It's like being the shy kid, at school, overhearing a conversation that excites you. But not knowing how to jump in.

The men and women having that conversation seem like giants, to me. And I, I still feel like a kid. I fear revealing my own naïveté, since there are aspects of the conversation that I don't have the background to comprehend. And I fear that once that is exposed, I'll lose the chance to participate, and be left playing with the toys that others create. Like, I read an article the other day about this study with rhesus monkeys. Researchers implanted electrodes into the monkeys' brains that allowed them to control virtual devices, and the animals developed the ability to manipulate a computer cursor using only their thoughts. Fascinating, how the brain seems to be inherently equipped to accept new interfaces. It implies so much that is exciting, and terrifying, and barely discovered, all by itself. A great deal is coming of this research, just this. It's transformational, this discovery. It's revealing that perhaps every neuron in our brain is a hand, able to shake hands with the universe. That our senses have been merely the best our bodies could offer. And it compels me to think I may be able to sense you in other ways, than the ways we have sensed each other, so far.

I imagine our son, growing in your womb, and the world he'll be unleashed into. None of this is scary, though some fear the consequences. It's all beautiful, the elegant programming of this universe. So beautiful, all of it.

See you tonight, sugar.

-Sam

TWENTY-ONE

TO MARK ONE YEAR WITHOUT SAM, I WILL HAUNT our favourite place tonight, the Hotel Rialto, where we stayed on New Year's Eve in 2010 and many birthdays and anniversaries in the years that followed. The kids are spending the night at my sister's house. I've booked a room for one.

I went on another internet date this morning. Why? I have no idea. I've been compulsively wandering the halls of OkCupid again lately. It's comforting, scrolling through profiles. Part of me believes I'll find Sam there, that we can start from the beginning.

What's your kid's favourite cartoon?

My date's name was Markus, and unlike with other dates, I felt completely calm and relaxed before meeting him. I didn't really care if I liked him, if he liked me.

An excerpt from his profile:

I am allergic to stupid. If you don't know the difference between "you're" and "your," chances are we
will find little in common. If you are vain, shallow,
weak-willed, or concerned with trends surrounding
pop culture, I will actively despise you. If you read the
word "Wilde" and think "girls gone" and not "Oscar,"
we should never meet.

I advised him that I do indeed enjoy pop culture, that I
am unapologetically vain, shallow, and weak-willed, and that
Oscar Wilde is fine but seems far too pleased with himself all
the time. He still wanted to meet. I insisted we schedule for late
morning, because I wanted to get it over with, check in to the
hotel, and have a nap before my *real* date, the most romantic
date of all, where I would stuff myself with haute cuisine and
chocolate cake in the fancy hotel restaurant, retire to my room,
and masturbate frantically in clean white linens to photos of
Sam, and fall asleep watching CNN.

I'm wearing a green cardigan, he texted at 9:30 a.m.

Great, will you still be wearing the green cardigan at 11:00?

*Affirmative, m'lady. I very much look forward to making your
acquaintance in person.*

Ditto.

○

"Hi. Markus?"

"Why, hello, m'lady." He had a British accent, which I
wasn't expecting.

His shoulder-length hair was parted neatly down the middle and brushed to a shine, a contrast to his patchy, unkempt

neckbeard. The green cardigan was cute, though. I ordered a latte and sat down across from him at the uncomfortably tiny bistro table he had chosen.

"So, you're an accountant, right?"

"Yes, that is correct." He smiled. His teeth were sharp and beige.

"Do you enjoy your work?"

"I do ... *not!* No, I actually barely tolerate it. But I must admit, it's better than astrophysics."

I laughed politely. He looked insulted.

"Oh, sorry," I said. "Have you had much experience with astrophysics?"

"I was getting my Ph.D. at Princeton. I left the program."

"Oh, wow. Why?"

"I wanted to move to Canada, where I was conceived. My mother is Canadian."

"You wanted to come here because you were conceived here? Like, because your parents had intercourse here?"

"Successful intercourse. They made *me.*"

"Right. Wow, I've never heard that before as a reason to move somewhere. That's neat."

"Where would you move to, if you moved to where you were conceived?"

"New York City."

"How stereotypical."

"I don't think so, actually — is it?"

"Undoubtedly."

"Huh, I never knew that."

"Actually, I'm talking about your name. Elsie. It rhymes with Chelsea, the neighbourhood in New York City. Why did they name you Elsie and not Chelsea? It's a bit of an old-fashioned name, isn't it? *Elsie.* It doesn't suit you much. You should tell your parents they were late to the name by about fifty years, ha!"

"I can't. They're dead."

"Oh, terribly sorry for your losses, then. I should have said 'Elsie' was a sophisticated and worldly choice. Forgive me."

"It's fine."

"So, what are you planning for the weekend? Any interest in taking a ride out to the peninsula in my Dodge Charger? It can travel up to two-hundred-and-three miles per hour, but don't worry. I wouldn't go full speed with you right away."

"Wow, fast. Um, I'm not sure. I'm busy with my kids pretty much all the time."

"I just had it custom painted. Cherry red with black racing stripes."

"Cool."

"You're partial to understatement, aren't you?"

"Sorry?"

"Conversation recap: You said, 'cool.' *I* said you must be partial to understatement. And I can assure you, it's beyond 'cool.' It is, as they say, a breathtaking ride. Perhaps you share that in common with my car?"

"Um."

"Sorry, got carried away."

"Yeah. Why don't you tell me about astrophysics?"

He sighed. "I have wholly extracted myself from that world. It's a bore."

"What did you study, specifically?"

"Fractal galaxy clusters."

"What does that mean?"

"I focused specifically on the fractal behaviour of high-mass galaxy structures, if you must know. I expect that means nothing to you."

"It sounds cool."

" '*Cool*,' once again, is not the word I would use, though it's cute when you say it. But let's move on, shall we?"

"My partner was a scientist," I said. "He was finishing his Ph.D. in computer science when he died. He was studying artificial intelligence."

"Oh. Well, once again, my condolences."

"I'm actually still in love with him. He's my son's father. I have a daughter, too, from my first marriage, and a stepson from Sam, but my stepson moved away with his mom when Sam died. Sam was the love of my life. He was brilliant and hilarious."

"Right-o. Thank you for sharing."

"You're welcome. Why did you leave Princeton?"

"I came to loathe academia. Numbers are much simpler. I supervise payroll clerks now."

His parents, back in England, had bought him a subscription to the *Journal of Astrophysics*, he said, but they were all sitting in a pile under his coffee table, where they would remain until he collected enough of them to start a bonfire.

He wasn't the worst creep I've ever met, even if he was pompous and condescending and talked mainly to my breasts. I wondered what had happened to turn him into the creature before me. Probably it was a combination of genius and repeated rejection. Sometimes a brilliant mind and a lack of self-awareness can produce a humble, quirky genius like Sam, someone generous with their intellect, someone with bottomless curiosity about others. But when a person is told all their life that they possess a brilliance so singular, so rare, that they are meant to innovate and inspire all the world with their dazzling mind, and when the world does not comply, a Markus emerges, with all the hallmark characteristics of a super-villain but none of the power or charisma. Notwithstanding the green cardigan.

Now he is telling my breasts about driving his car over the Malahat and how fast it shoots past all the other vehicles climbing the hill.

"I'm so sorry, but I just realized I have to go now."

"Oh, so soon? May I walk you to your vehicle?"

"Yeah, okay."

On the walk, he said he looked forward to seeing me sitting in his passenger seat with my hair blowing in the breeze. My wince was uncontainable, but he didn't pick up on my very strong discomfort cues, and in fact followed me all the way around to my car door, lunging at me with a hug that I did not have time to wiggle away from.

"So, this weekend?"

"I'm extremely busy with my kids, so ..."

"Right, brilliant. I look forward to it, m'lady."

○

I don't belong in restaurants like this anymore. The eatery at the Hotel Rialto is called Veneto, and it's an elegant place with crazy-high ceilings and a midcentury modern hipster vibe. I've completely let myself go since getting back from Calgary, since Ada May died, since my sister and I stopped speaking. It's remarkable how much weight a person can gain in three weeks of eating ten thousand calories a day and lying on the couch. My pants are ill fitting, and though I haven't eaten yet I can feel the thick of my stomach pushing against my waistband. My bum, which has always been a relatively firm size XL, is now a wide, soft moon of rippled cheese, and at present it is drooping over both sides of my chair.

A group of polished young women, drenched in various musky perfumes, is seated at the table next to me, their hair all piles of shining waves.

They start taking selfies. It's thrilling.

"Oh God, erase that," says one woman, whose physical beauty is nearly painful to behold.

"Yeah, we look, like, all derpy. Here, let's do another one."

They duck-lip and squinch for the phone.

Now they're talking about depositions and demand letters. Lawyers. I have a sudden urge to make friends with them. Maybe if I lean over and whisper something lawyerly? *Magna Carta*, I could say, and then I could give them a wink. They would probably invite me to join their table, and we could take selfies together and talk about penises and politics and fashion.

I order a virgin cocktail, a plate of calamari, a bowl of mussels, roasted rutabaga with sake kasu emulsion, a chicken leg with celery root and juniper sauce, and a slice of caramel chocolate cake.

"Oh, are you waiting for someone? Do you need another set of cutlery?"

"Nope, it's all for me!"

"Okay, excellent. And I'll make sure to bring it out one plate at a time."

"Can you bring it all at once?"

"Everything at once? Are you sure?"

"Yes, I'm sure."

I want to see all the food laid out before me. I want to feel like a rich giant who lives in a castle in the clouds, surveying my feasting table with greedy, beady eyes. *Fee fi fo fum*, I say to myself as no fewer than four servers arrive at my table with the contents of my personal buffet.

At this hour on December 6, 2015 — one year ago tonight — Sam was still very much alive, and I was going out of my mind wondering where the hell he was.

O

Hey, dinner's ready, you on your way?

Yeah, just looking for a new coil for my vape. My coil burned out.

Ok, what's your ETA?

45 mins

K, see you soon

O

I was struggling that night, really struggling. The drinking had become so disruptive and frightening that I'd applied to a co-op a few days earlier and was preparing to sign the papers and move out if he refused to go to rehab. In fact, I was planning on issuing an ultimatum that night, which was why I'd cooked a nice dinner. I would approach the subject as gently but firmly as possible. I'd researched rehab centres, had made phone calls to his mom to discuss logistics; I was fully prepared to calmly and lovingly proceed with a separation if he chose not to go. It wasn't what I wanted, but it was necessary. I'd been feeling ambivalent about it for weeks, but we'd gone on a date night to SilverCity Cinema the night before, and that had clinched it: I was done.

It had been our first date night in a long time. His cousin Rebecca, a med student at the local university, came over to babysit the kids. I got dressed up, put on makeup. He shaved, wore a dress shirt and his favourite paperboy cap.

"You look handsome," I said, standing in line at the concession.

"You look beautiful."

I leaned my head against his chest and slid my hand under his jacket and around his waist. A mickey of vodka fell out of the inside pocket and landed between us and the couple in front of us.

"No!" I shouted reflexively.

He grinned at them.

"Whoops! Forgot I had that." He tried to slide it back in his pocket.

"Can you just throw that in the garbage, please?"

"No, I'll go pour it out. I'll pour it down the drain, I promise. I have to go to the bathroom anyways. Meet you in the theatre." He kissed my forehead, shoved a fistful of bills and coins into my hand, and left me standing there mortified, trying to avoid further eye contact with the couple by feigning passionate interest in the concession menu.

I bought popcorn and licorice and a Diet Coke, headed into the theatre, and found the perfect pair of aisle seats in an empty section, but then a group of rowdy teenage boys came barrelling in and sat right in front of me.

Sam arrived, gave me another apologetic head kiss, grabbed a handful of popcorn, and put his big, warm hand on my knee. *This will actually be good*, I thought. *We will watch* Mockingjay Part 2 *in this movie theatre, and then we will go home, and he will lovingly pummel my cervix, and then we will talk until 2:00 a.m., just like the old days.*

The group of boys in front of us was making teenage idiot sounds, throwing popcorn at each other, making fun of the previews. My anxiety spiked slightly, remembering those same types of boys snapping my bra, asking me if my pussy was wet on the bus, throwing pennies on the ground and saying, *You dropped your pocket.* I reassured myself that I was old enough now to be invisible to them. They would be annoying, rude little assholes, but they would ignore us.

Five minutes into the actual movie, the opening credits still onscreen, I felt Sam's hand slide off my knee. I looked at him. His head was flopped all the way forward. I shook him awake, and he cleared his throat.

"Sorry, was ju*ssss* tired furra*minnnn,*" he slurred.

"You're *drunk,*" I whispered. "You drank that vodka, didn't you?"

But he had already passed out again, slumped all the way down in his seat. He was snoring loudly.

I put my mouth right up to his ear and whispered through my teeth. "Wake *up.* Wake up right *now,* Sam!"

"Yes, yes, darling," he muttered in his sleep, just as he would do when I woke up in the mornings. "I'm coming, I'm coming. I'll be right there."

"Dude, check out the old guy behind us. He's all fucked up, hahahahaha."

Sam was still slumped, still snoring, totally oblivious to what had become of him. The humiliation was all mine.

I got up, brushed the popcorn off my boobs, grabbed my purse, and left.

"*Fuck* you, *fuck* you, *fuck* you," I hissed under my breath the whole way to the car. I got in, strangled the steering wheel, and scream-sobbed for about five minutes before pulling myself together, starting the ignition, and making my way out of the underground parking lot. I was going home. I didn't care what happened to him. The movie theatre could call the police, for all I cared, and if the police called me to pick him up, I would tell them to take him to the drunk tank.

As I was about to turn out of the complex, a person staggered up and slammed their body against the passenger door.

I rolled down the window. "Get. In."

He got in.

"Mmm'*srry*, darling."

"Don't talk to me."

"You mad?"

"Do *not* talk to me. Do not say another word."

He started to cry. Deep, pathetic blubbering that made me even angrier.

"Stop it," I snapped.

We pulled into the driveway. He wobbled into the house.

"Go to bed," I said.

He went to bed.

His cousin was baffled by our being home.

"Sam got sick," I said. "We had to call it a night so he could lie down."

I wasn't covering for him; I just didn't want his twenty-year-old cousin to be traumatized.

"I hope everything's okay," she said. "Tell Sam to feel better."

"Thanks so much for coming tonight. I'll call you a cab, okay?"

"Sure. We'll do a rain check."

"Rain check, definitely."

TWENTY-TWO

I'VE HAD ONLY TWO PIECES OF CALAMARI, ONE MUSSEL, a forkful of chicken, and two bites of chocolate caramel cake when an abrupt and overwhelming nausea comes over me. I have to sit absolutely still or I will vomit on the beautiful lawyers and ruin their outfits and hairstyles.

I look at my phone: 7:45.

Very gingerly, so as not to barf all over the gleaming marble floors, I leave my table and find a hostess.

"Hi. I have to go now. That's my table over there with the cloud giant's feast, but I can't eat anything now because I feel like I'm going to puke."

"Oh no! Can I get it wrapped up for you?"

"No. I have to lie down. I'm staying in room three-ten. Can the food just be charged to my room?"

"Of course! Sure you don't want it wrapped up?"

"I'm sure. Thank you."

I am dizzy. I have to hold onto the wainscotting to get to the elevator.

In my room, I strip and crawl under the sheets, but the smell of bleached linens makes the nausea worse. I try holding my breath and keeping completely still, but it doesn't work. I have to roll out of bed and crawl to the toilet, where I expel a batch of snakes made up of at least a hundred dollars' worth of seafood, poultry, chocolate cake, and a full year of rage and sorrow and stupid, stupid broken dreams, puking and puking until it's only bile.

Then I eat some toothpaste, crawl back to the bed, and fall into a dream.

It's the dead woman, but this time she's even more life-like. Alive, even. She's pacing along the side of the SilverCity Cinema, checking her watch every few seconds, and she keeps peeking around the corner at the entrance. There is colour in her cheeks, and her eyes are no longer that rotting skim-milk shade. They are green eyes now.

"What are you doing?" I ask her. I know she can't see me, since I am an invisible floating dream orb, but she seems to hear me.

"I'm waiting for him," she mumbles impatiently.

"For who?"

She doesn't respond. She has spotted something, and she starts toward it like a cat.

And there he is. Sam, my Sam, tumbling out of the theatre's revolving door and landing on his face.

She rushes to him, helps him up.

"Mmm'*srry*, darling," he mumbles.

She takes him in her arms and holds him. She looks into the drunken swirls of his eyes with a love so pure and expansive that the last of her deadness begins to disappear, the purple spider veins on her forehead vanishing.

"Shhh," she says, stroking his face, kissing his lips. "Shhh, it's okay. I'm here now, Sam, I'm here. I've got you, love."

O

I wake up at 10:30 p.m. to my phone buzzing. It's a text:
Hello, m'lady, thinking of you XOXO.
Ew.
The nausea is gone, but another wave comes when I remember Markus the astrophysicist incel with his shiny, middle-parted hair.
I get up for a glass of water, brush my teeth.
"What are you doing?" the mirror says.
"I'm sad."
"You look terrible. You should go down to the bar and find someone to talk to. That will make you feel better."
"Good idea."

O

The bartender's name is Ahmed.
"I recognize you," I say, leaning my elbows on the bar.
"Oh?"
"I remember your handlebar moustache. My spouse really admired it. We used to come here sometimes, to drink expensive cocktails and pretend we were rich."
"You and everyone else in town."
"But then he died of a drug overdose last year, so ... Oh well."
"Shit. I'm so sorry, dude. Can I get you a drink?"
"No, thanks. I just came to say hello. I'm staying here at the hotel by myself, because it's the deathiversary. I ordered three

hundred dollars' worth of food from the restaurant, but then I felt like I was going to puke, so I had a nap instead."

"Okay. Well, thanks for saying hello. I'm sorry about your partner. I'm glad he liked my moustache."

"He admired it. He was getting his Ph.D. in computer science, studying artificial intelligence and machine learning and stuff."

"Wow. That's impressive."

"I know. I didn't know he was using drugs. I thought he was just an alcoholic. I only found out about the drugs from the toxicology report."

"I'm really sorry. Sure I can't get you a drink?"

"No, the last time I drank, I ended up cradling my partner's Death Star cookie-jar urn and scream-crying at my mother-in-law's house in Calgary, and that really scared her dog."

"Well, we don't want a repeat of that."

"No. Do you have a girlfriend?"

"I have a husband."

"Do you love him?"

"Of course! Very much. His name is Adam. He's a physiotherapist."

"Oh. I could use some therapy."

"He's a physio, so he helps people with movement and exercise, but I can give you his card if you want."

"No thanks. Anyway, I have to go smoke now, so bye."

○

It's pouring rain and I don't have an umbrella. My cigarette is getting all wet and sad.

I walk across the street to Centennial Square. There are homeless people in sleeping bags under the archway and a few teenagers sharing an umbrella and milling around the water fountain, vaping.

I approach the teenagers. "Excuse me, but do you sell drugs?"

A girl with thick black eyeliner and fishnets laughs. "What?"

"Do you sell drugs?"

"*No.* Do you?"

"No. Who sells the drugs around here?"

"What do you mean 'the drugs'?" They all laugh.

"I'm just looking for the person who sold my husband drugs on this night last year. He overdosed and died. I'd like to find the person and ask them to apologize to me."

She laughs again.

"I don't think she's joking," a boy says.

"Oh, wait, are you not joking?"

"No. Never mind."

I know it's preposterous, but I had a vision of finding the culprit tonight, the fucker who sold Sam the poison that took him. I had a vision of telling him what he's done to my life, demanding an apology. We need an apology, all of us overdose-crisis Left-Behinds, huddling separately and invisibly on our little makeshift island. Stigmatized, unacknowledged, drenched in the shame of our dead loves. I consider walking up Pandora Avenue to canvas the people hanging around outside the church, but I'm completely soaked now, and frankly I have no energy left for further detective work. Instead, I walk to Burger King and order a Whopper, which was Sam's favourite food. I eat it in a booth across from a blind woman, wondering if she senses that she is seated opposite the shittiest, loneliest, saddest person alive. Then I go to 7-Eleven and fill two plastic baggies with eleven dollars' worth of penny candies.

Back in the hotel room, I open my laptop.

I've figured it out. The dead woman can't be a coincidence. She is me, I am her. I know what I have to do now.

I go to Craigslist and post the following ad in the Gigs section:

ISO WIZARD FOR SPACE-TIME TRAVEL

Hello:

I am seeking an experienced, efficient, and principled wizard to assist me in locating a wormhole. Must have experience with quantum-jumping and the safe navigation of antimatter worlds. December 5, 2015, is where I need to be, so the world I'm jumping into needs to be as identical to this one as possible. My objective is to prevent a catastrophe and assume the position of my parallel self while safely and compassionately disposing of her. Pay negotiable, but please consider a valuable coupon for housework and hugs as down payment.

SERIOUS REPLIES ONLY. THANKS.

Do NOT contact me with unsolicited services or offers.

TWENTY-THREE

I CAN SAFELY SAY I'VE CIRCLED BACK TO THE DEPRES-
sion phase recently. The depression is worse than the anger, because at least in anger, I had energy. My life force has dwindled.
I am slovenly and slow-minded and forgetful. On the bright
side, the insomnia has completely disappeared. Sleep has become my new best friend. If someone told me I could just go to
bed and never wake up, I would kiss them passionately, put on
my PJs, and bid the world night-night forever.

That said, I have at the same time developed a new
semi-conscious hobby of spending hours every evening making hateful faces into my phone, overlain with bunny noses
and cat eyes. I'm like a fairy-tale villain, only instead of magic
mirrors, I have Snapchat as my looking glass. What I find
so compelling about this app is that it can take my face, the
most forlorn and beaten-down face on this island, and turn it
into a blemish-free, bright-eyed supermodel face *with* whis-
kers. Aside from the obligations of daily life — parenting,

bare-minimum cleaning, finding food — Snapchat and Candy Crush are the only two things in my world that inspire me to stay awake for any length of time. Everything else feels meh, except the possibility of a real-life wizard responding to my Craigslist ad.

So far I've had only one response:

From: Hyacinth Kohl <f4dd500067e433f-
280f7193831ca586e@reply.craigslist.org>

Date: December 9, 2016 at 1:40 p.m.

Subject: Re: ISO WIZARD FOR SPACE-TIME TRAVEL

To: xk6c2-5765853262@gigs.craigslist.org

This dimension is super boring. My soul aches for adventure. Can I come with you and bring my bearded
dragon if I help you jump?

Super boring, huh? I compose then abandon a reply to Hyacinth Kohl, explaining that I am not looking for a new friend to commiserate about how dull life can be, but that I am in *actual psychic pain*, the likes of which she can probably not even conceive of, and that I need an *actual wizard* who can help me jump through space-time to rescue Sam.

Everything in my life is objectively terrible. My sister is still not returning my calls. Ada May is dead, and I am consumed with guilt over not even bothering to say goodbye (even if I was just another Marge, and even though she would probably have gone to France if I were dying). Also, I humiliated myself in front of Saul, the only man I've ever been as attracted to as Sam. Also, I am a terrible mother who is unable to be in the moment with my children because I am consumed with examining the horrific train wreck my life has become and fantasizing about getting out of it somehow.

I am currently at the swimming pool, waiting for my kids to finish their lessons. The air is thick with salt 'n' vinegar chip particles and chlorine. I am blasting "Cosmic Dancer" by T. Rex on my headphones and staring at the hairy old guys sitting on the edge of the hot tub, muttering Italian to each other. I like that they all have exactly the same cute, round bellies.

My phone buzzes.

Hello, m'lady. Fancy meeting me for a drink tonight?

This fucking guy. Speaking of objectively terrible things, it's been a week since the coffee shop date and he just won't give up.

I can't, my kids have lessons and then bed. Have a nice night.

What kind of lessons?

I start composing an unambiguous *Piss off, not interested* message, but then the kids are out of the pool, Benji climbing over the rope into the towel on my lap.

"Can we get kiddo meals tonight? Please?"

I'm too tired to contemplate throwing yet another frozen pizza into the oven, so I agree that kiddo meals are a good plan. Things cannot possibly get worse than they are right now, so why not just embrace the fact that I am probably just destined to be a bloated, exhausted slob who feeds her children kiddo meals all night long.

Halfway through our dining experience, a young mother approaches our table with her distressed-looking toddler.

"Hey," she says aggressively, "your son stole my daughter's doll."

She gestures to the mini Barbie doll on the table, the one I observed my son retrieve from his cardboard meal box and unwrap only moments ago.

"Oh, this? This came with the kiddo meal. He just opened it. Maybe your daughter has the same one?"

"No, my daughter brought that doll from home. That doll is *not* a kiddo meal toy. That toy came from our house."

Her daughter is now frantic.

"That's my toy," she's shrieking. "My Barbie!"

"Okay," I say. "But, actually, it is a kiddo meal toy. He just unwrapped it, see?" I hold up the plastic wrapper.

"My Barbie, Mummy! *Mine.*"

"Hey," I say to the mom, "no problem. Just take this one, no worries."

She won't take it. She picks up her daughter and huffs off, muttering loudly about how *some* people just *steal* things.

"It's okay, Neveah, some people are just bad people, and they steal other people's things. Shh, don't worry, sweetheart. That little boy is just a rude little boy."

As she's strapping her kid into the stroller, another voice pipes up from across the atrium of the pigpen. It is a mom with neat blond hair, sitting with her linebacker-type husband and a trio of boys in buzz cuts and polo shirts.

"That's not a kiddo meal toy," she declares to the entire room. "Kiddo meal toys are Nerf guns."

She is now standing up and showcasing a Nerf gun toy like she's Vanna White. She even looks like Vanna White — she's glossy and lithe, impeccably put together in a white peacoat and matte leather boots that go up to her thighs.

"All my boys got Nerf guns in their kiddo meals, see?"

Exhibit A, Nerf gun.

"Nerf guns are the kiddo meal toys for boys, not Barbies," she continues. Now she's narrowing her eyes and addressing me directly. "You are teaching your kids to steal and lie, lady.

Nice parenting. Good job. Good for you, making that little girl cry."

"But, Mama," my ten-year-old daughter whispers urgently across the table, her eyes filling with tears, "the Barbie is a kiddo meal toy. Benji just got it. I saw him unwrap it."

"I know."

All the other patrons have suddenly roused from their sleepy Soylent cud-chewing. They are looking gleefully from her to me to her, amazed at their good fortune at having stumbled into a live courtroom drama.

I know how this looks. I know I should defend my kid or leave, but I can't think properly. I am paralyzed.

fast food

pigpen

sweatpants

fast food

pigpen

sweatpants

That's all that comes to mind.

I look at my children. Their hair is wet from the pool. They're both in their pyjamas. I am dressed in stained sweatpants and a T-shirt that says *CIBC Run for the Cure: Bye-Bye Boobies 2016!* My hair is a fright of frizz. I'm in three-day-old, blotted eyeliner.

We are *those* people. Trash people.

"I mean, who allows their kid to steal another kid's toy?" the blond woman clucks theatrically to the people next to her.

Beside me, a grandma is hand-feeding cheeseburgers to her identical twin grandsons. I look at her beseechingly for support. She purses her lips and averts her eyes.

I hear Sam's voice in my head, kind and calm. *Get the kids together and go home, sweetheart. Just get the fuck out of here; you don't need this. This means nothing. Go.*

I'm not listening to you, I think back at him. *You don't know anything about my life now. I would never have come here if it wasn't for you. There would be no kiddo-meal-toy trial if it weren't for you, so you don't get to tell me what to do.*

"I'll be right back. Watch your brother."

I ask the teenage boy at the counter if I can please purchase a new Barbie kiddo meal toy.

"Just on its own?"

"Yeah."

He reaches under the register and hands me a new doll, still in the package.

"That blond lady over there is saying my son stole another kid's toy, and he didn't." I feel sure that he will be on my side if he understands the scourge of injustice unfolding in the pigpen. "They were saying there were no kiddo meal Barbies, and there are!"

"Huh."

"It's that lady over there — that one," I say, pointing out the blond.

He smiles piteously. "Good luck, ma'am."

I realize that my breathing is ragged.

I make my way back to the pigpen enclosure, clutching the packaged Barbie, and as I open the door, the blond lady is standing right in front of me. I hold up the Barbie triumphantly.

"See?" I say. "This is for a kiddo meal! It's the exact same Barbie my son just got, and the same one that little girl must have had."

I am hoping for an apology, or at the very least a truce.

Nope.

"Doesn't prove anything." She sniffs.

Then she does the thing that some people do when they want to belittle another person.

She looks me up and then down and then up again. And then she smirks. It feels like a smirk about my entire being, my mothering, about my children, the integrity of their little beings.

Both of my kids are still sitting at the table. My son is oblivious, happily crunching his chemical apple slices, but my daughter is staring across the room at me with an expression of pubescent terror.

I take a deep breath, wishing I had a mouth full of ketchup so I could squirt it at Nerf Gun Mom's white wool coat, but all I have is this beautiful package of Barbie and the truth.

I duck behind her, making like I'm going to slink back to my chair, but as I am doing so, and very, very quietly, and very tenderly, I whisper in her ear, "*You are a fucking cunt.*"

She goes bananas.

"Ex-*cuse* me? What did you just say to me?"

My daughter's eyes look like they are about to pop out of her face.

"Pardon?" I ask, smiling politely.

"What did you just say to me?"

"I didn't say anything."

"How dare you use that kind of language in a child's play area! What kind of a person are you?"

"I'm Elsie Jane," I say.

Her hands are on her hips now. "I didn't ask your name; I asked what kind of a person says the C-word in the kiddo play area!"

"I'm just a person enjoying a nice burger in the pigpen," I say.

"Oh, now you're calling me a pig? Oh wow, now I've heard it all. Wow, just wow. Nice example you're setting for your kids, bitch!"

My daughter is crying and shaking.

"Why is the lady yelling at you, Mama? My mom didn't do anything," she sobs.

Everyone in the pigpen is now gawking at the elegant blond Nerf Gun Mom who is absolutely losing her shit at me, the dowdy, unkempt Barbie Thief Mom. I feel the zeitgeist turning in my favour.

The grandma of the twins pipes up: "You should sit down, dear," she says to Nerf Gun Mom, who zips up her coat aggressively at me and spits, "You think you're a tough woman? I could beat the shit out of you."

I put my coat on, gather up my children, and leave.

Good job, darling, says Sam, but I am not proud.

In the car, I check my phone. Seven new text messages.

6:22 p.m. *Elsie, allow me the pleasure of your company this weekend.*

6:27 p.m. *You only live once ;)*

6:40 p.m. *Give me a chance. Let me win your favour. You won't regret it.*

6:59 p.m. *How's this for a cheesy pickup line: "I hail from a constitutional monarchy; let me make you my Canadian princess."*

7:21 p.m. *I told my father about you the other night. He is excited for me.*

7:39 p.m. *Hello?*

7:45 p.m. *Hello?!!!??*

This can't go on. I have to put an end to it.

Hi Markus, just need to let you know that I've decided I'm not ready to date. I'm too busy with my kids, and still grieving my partner who passed away last year. It was nice meeting you, and good luck out there.

I block him.

Fortunately, when I arrive home, there's a palate cleanser in my inbox:

From: Zulobian Qa <e5ccfe9ef6423794b8fe981b
cba231e8@reply.craigslist.org>

Date: December 9, 2016 at 3:53 a.m.

Subject: Re: ISO WIZARD FOR SPACE-TIME TRAVEL

To: xk6c2-5765853262@gigs.craigslist.org

Greetings! It is I, Zulobian Qa, talented wizard at your service. The task you describe is a simple one, space-time-wise. One problem: the moon's location on 5 DEC 2015? No, it is all wrong. Too hard to get you there intact, unless you don't mind arriving in bits and pieces. I will send you there on 8 DEC 2015 instead, and it must be after 7:51 p.m. PST.

Now, one more thing: I have plenty of druidenium minerals, but you must understand that they are expensive. "Coupons for housework and hugs" is not an acceptable substitute for payment. Consult the wizard wage grid and you will see that a journeyman will not charge less than a 400-oz brick of gold for a task of this nature.

-Zulobian Qa

Zulobian Qa is not taking this seriously. I consider deleting the ad, but end up deleting my OkCupid account instead, remembering how Markus has ruined all the whimsy there for me.

Things are just getting worse and worse.

Why on earth should I stay here?

TWENTY-FOUR

OVER AND OVER, I REPLAY THAT NIGHT.

"Where have you been?"

"I told you, I was buying a coil for my vape."

"Until eleven thirty on a Sunday night?"

"Okay, okay, I met some university kids downtown, and we went to the Breakwater to smoke some weed and watch the sunset."

"It's been pouring rain. There was no sunset, and you're not even wet."

"No, there was a sunset, and it was so beautiful! Please, darling, let's go down there and smoke pot and watch the sunset together one night. It's so peaceful!"

My plan to issue the ultimatum was going to have to wait until another night. He was acting loopy and euphoric. His voice had a strange crackle to it, and he kept pawing at me and trying to kiss me.

"I have to go to bed now."

"Just watch this one YouTube video with me. Please? It's beautiful. You'll like it."

The video was of a young man working as a cashier at Walmart. He was trying not to cry, so the customer at the checkout asked if he was okay. At first he said yes, but then his lower lip began to quiver violently.

"My mother committed suicide last night," he sobbed.

"Aw, honey," said the customer. She put her purse down on the counter, went behind the checkout, and took him in her arms. He was weeping and weeping.

Sam was beaming creepily as he watched me take it all in.

"This is really disturbing. Why did you want me to watch this?"

"Because it's beautiful!"

"It's not beautiful; it's devastating. I'm going to bed."

"There can be beauty in devastation, you know!" he called after me.

I went down to bed. He came down, too, looking for his sleep mask, unable to find it.

"I guess I'm sleeping in the spare room tonight?" He seemed hopeful that I would say no and invite him to stay in our bed.

"Yes." I sighed.

"I understand. Okay. Well, good night, darling. I love you."

"I love you, too. Good night."

I could have at least said *It's okay, sleep with me tonight* before he kissed me good night and climbed the stairs. If he'd been next to me in bed, I could have sensed him in distress, because maybe he made noises, right? Maybe he struggled and called for me, and what if I'd been right there, right beside him? I could have done CPR and called 911. I would have been furious, waking up the baby and following the ambulance to the hospital, but it could have been a wake-up call, his rock bottom, the slap in the face he needed to realize that he had to bite the bullet and go to treatment. Instead, I let him climb the stairs. He stayed up for a while. I heard him pour himself a drink, go out for a cigarette, heard the patio door swing open and shut.

I went to bed alone. I fell asleep.

The next morning in the kitchen, I noticed an uncorked bottle of wine on the counter, still almost full. Odd, because Sam would never open a bottle without emptying it, but I brushed it off. He must have been tired and fallen asleep.

I showered, got Benji dressed, made his lunch. Usually, I would kiss Sam goodbye. *Have a great day*, I'd say, and he'd murmur, *You too, darling.* Benji would kiss him, too. *Wave bye to Dada.*

I didn't kiss him goodbye that day. Something stopped me. I lingered outside the door of the spare bedroom, Benji on my hip, his daycare backpack and my purse flung over my shoulder. If I had opened that door, I would have found Sam dead. According to the autopsy, he died at approximately 2:30 a.m.

That whole morning, while I was getting ready, he was dead. While I poured Cheerios and puttered in the kitchen, he was dead. While I showered, while I blow-dried my hair, while I squeezed my blackheads in the mirror and applied mascara, he was dead. While I sang the "Skinnamarink" song and rolled socks onto Benji's sausage feet, Sam was dead. While I dropped Benji off at daycare, grabbed coffee at a drive-through before work, waved at the office parkade attendant, he was dead. All day, he was dead, and I had no idea, no inkling, until I called his office and they said he hadn't shown up, that they'd been worried, too. That was the moment when the terrible knowing slithered through me.

I told you, sometimes you just know things, and I just knew. But before I knew? Before I knew, I was a blissful, normal, stupid, lucky fool all fucking day while Sam was lying dead in the spare bedroom.

O

It was the police who found him. I called my sister from my office. I called her because of the terrible knowing, and I didn't want to go home. If the terrible knowing was real, I didn't want to be the one to find him.

I called my sister. I said, "There's something wrong. He wouldn't not call work. He wouldn't not let them know he wasn't coming in. He'd never do that."

She said, "Maybe his phone died and he's not feeling well enough to charge it."

She said not to worry, because he'd been weird lately, right?

She sent the police to my place to check on him. A wellness check, she called it.

"I'm sure he's fine," she said. "You just come to my place."

And when I got to her house and there was a knock on the door, she said it was just the pizza guy, but it wasn't the pizza guy at all. She was wrong. There was an officer at the door.

He was wearing a blue police uniform. He had blond hair and a sharp nose and a radio clipped on his belt. He told me to sit on the couch. He kneeled before me, like he was about to propose.

I was already saying, *No, no, no*, and fleeing the room before he could say, "I'm very sorry." My sister followed me to the kitchen, took me by the shoulders, turned me around, guided me back to the living room.

"You need to sit down, Elsie," she said. "Sit down. Sit."

I sat down. A good dog. I put a couch cushion over my face so I didn't have to look at the officer when he started talking again.

"We found a deceased male in the upstairs bedroom. He was in bed, under the covers."

I threw the pillow at the wall and tried to dive through the floor then. I don't remember making noise, but I must have been. I must have been making all kinds of bad noises, because the officer said, "Hey, try to calm down, okay? We don't want to scare the kids. I know it's hard. I know it's hard, but your screaming is scaring the kids. See? Your baby is scared. He's crying. I know it's hard, but you have to calm down."

"What happened?" I sobbed. "What fucking happened?"

"I'm sorry, but I don't know," the officer said. "The coroner will call you. I'll need to ask you a few questions to verify his identity now, okay? You let me know when you're ready. I need to know his full name and his date of birth."

"I'm not ready. What fucking happened?"

○

The coroner called the next day. I was sitting on my sister's couch, staring at the wall, while everyone was watching *Seinfeld*.

"My name is Lorna Beeker. I'm the coroner."

Lorna the Coroner didn't know what had happened to Sam, either. Lorna was brusque and disdainful. She spoke to me like I was her hundredth phone idiot of the day. No empathy, no warmth, no acknowledgement that this phone call felt like a dog ripping out my larynx. Lorna was all business.

"I will be doing an autopsy," she said. "Do you know what that means?"

"What?"

"Do you understand what an autopsy is."

"I —"

"It means I will be examining the body to look for evidence of disease or injury."

The body?

It had been less than twenty-four hours since I'd found out Sam was dead. None of it was real. Lorna the Coroner was still talking, but I was stuck on *the body.*

The body. The body. The body.

Somebody was sobbing. It was me. It was interrupting Lorna and making her cross.

"Is there someone else there you can put on the phone who isn't crying and will actually understand what I'm saying?"

I handed the phone to my sister, went out to the car, drove to the corner store, and bought my first pack of cigarettes in five years.

O

In the end, the autopsy didn't show anything.

"We will be doing a toxicology report," the coroner said in her second call to me. She was softer this time. "It can take a few months. We are quite overloaded right now with illicit drug deaths."

"So it was an overdose? Was it alcohol?"

"Illicit drug poisoning is far more likely, statistically speaking."

"But he didn't use drugs. He drank. He was not a drug user. Marijuana, sometimes, but that's it."

"I'm afraid you're not the first person to be surprised that their family member was using. It happens all the time. More frequently than not, in fact."

"So will the toxicology report tell us exactly what he took?"

"It will provide a general picture, yes. We didn't find any substances at the scene of this death, so we can't test for fentanyl specifically, but we can look for opioid markers in the blood. As I say, the toxicology report will provide a general picture of what was in the system at the time of death. A *general* picture."

"Then how do you know how all these people are dying? Isn't there a fentanyl overdose crisis going on right now?"

"The report will provide you with a general picture of what was in the system at the time of death. As I've said."

"Okay, but what I'm asking you is, when will we know exactly what killed him? He was healthy."

"As I've said, the report will provide a general picture of what was in the system at the time of death. I am unable to speculate on the substance that caused his death at this time, but I will repeat that the autopsy did not demonstrate any disease or injury. In that sense, you're correct, he was healthy. Please wait for the toxicology report."

O

Sam and I should be living in Fairfield right now, in one of those character houses we loved, a few blocks from the ocean. He should be doing AI experiments in the attic, and I should be playing guitar in the study while the kids climb the kindly arbutus tree in the backyard. We should be having mundane fights and lazy, familiar, middle-aged sex. I mean, for fuck's sake, that's where I should be right now.

But no, I'm stuck in this life I despise. So what's keeping me here? Why shouldn't I figure out a way to escape this fresh, hot turd of a timeline? Speaking of which, there's also the matter of Markus, who has gifted me with a demonstration of how frighteningly entitled and insane some men can be and how I'm unlikely to find anyone to fall in love with ever again. The creep even tracked me down on Facebook and sent this message request:

Found you.

You are, if I may say so, a stupid cunt. I'm better off without you, obviously, but the way you misrepre- sented yourself online as available by going on a dating website infuriates me. Hot tip: dating web- sites are for people who actually want to date each other. You've ignored every gesture I've made to connect with you. My texts left unread, my email ignored. As if I'm some kind of creep, as if I'm worth- less. You have no manners and no integrity. I am a very patient and understanding man, but you've crossed a line and made me angry. You *will* regret this.

I had blocked his number and therefore had no idea what texts he was talking about, but then I remembered that I'd given him both my phone number *and* my email address, because I am an idiot. I opened my junk mail, and sure enough …

From: Markus <markus_your_gentleman@vergemail
.com>
Date: December 12, 2016 at 1:02 p.m.
Subject: Regret
To: Elsie J. <Elsiejane@vergemail.com>

I regret our paths ever crossed. In fact, I regret nothing more in the last ten years of my life.

 Before we met, I should have written this:

Dear Elsie Jane,
Thank you for the incredible gift of your phone
number. How privileged I feel, how blessed.
Unfortunately, I am not interested in having
you accompany me on any adventures, roman-
tic and erotic as they could turn out. You sense
that we could do extraordinary things together,
and your sense is correct. Regrettably, though
I know I could drive you to places you've never
been before, we simply aren't a good match.
* So, no, I will not meet you for coffee after all.*
Why, you ask?
* Because I am a hot rod, sleek and purpose*
built for speed. And you, Elsie, you're a jalopy,
limping along the side of the highway, farting
and spewing black smoke. You tried to flag me
down, but I don't stop for jalopies like you. I
have places to go. Maybe other smoking pieces
of ass will be worth stopping for. I wish you
luck, femoid, and I hope you know you're not
actually very pretty. Interesting-looking, sure,

but overall a 4/10.

Beep-beep,

-Markus

Working back from the email, I checked my blocked numbers, and sure enough, there were about thirty archived texts from his number, which varied in nature from pleading to sneering to vaguely threatening. I typed and erased a few *Fuck off, you entitled prick* responses into Messenger before ultimately deciding to just block him. I would try to forget about it, to focus on more urgent things, like Snapchat, Candy Crush, and especially quantum-jumping.

I decided on the night of the deathiversary that if I was going to engage in quantum-jumping to rescue Sam, I needed to do it right. Fortunately, as of tonight, my plan is *finally* beginning to unfold in the way I envisioned.

From: Ion <e4825ab1386a3c06953a58ea13df71a0@
reply.craigslist.org>
Date: December 20, 2016 at 1:02 p.m.
Subject: Re: ISO WIZARD FOR SPACE-TIME TRAVEL
To: xk6c2-5765853262@gigs.craigslist.org

I'm a professional wizard emeritus with certificates from all the necessary agencies, so you can rest assured in my efficiency and principles. I've done my 5,000 hours of quantum-jumping to be labelled a Master of the Quantum Fields. According to my devices, there are multiple "December 5, 2015"s nearby and safely accessible, with only minor discrepancies from the one we experienced here. Before I

agree to work with you, I'll need more details about
the nature of the catastrophe we'll be preventing.
Please be as specific as possible. I have a strict code
of ethics that cannot be broken under any circumstances. Please reply to this email address as I've
recently had to disconnect all of my phones, for the
standard reasons. If you don't know what those reasons are, we probably shouldn't work together.

Regards,

-Ion

Part of me recognizes how ridiculous this whole quantum-jumping plan would appear to an outsider. I also get that I have a choice, that I could pause now to examine my state of mind, that I could laugh at myself and settle back into material reality. But then what? Then it would all be more of the same. More Sauls. More Markuses. More fast-food pigpen fight scenarios. So you know what? I'm willing to risk making a fool of myself. I've spent hours reading about quantum cosmology — the many-worlds interpretation, universal wave function, quantum superposition — and here's what I've come to understand: Other worlds of you and me exist, the stories of our lives woven and split, woven and split, our subjective experiences simply swatches of fabric in the endlessly layered tapestry of space-time. Patterns of every conceivable colour and variation, every rhythmic and symbolic sequence imaginable: they all exist simultaneously. And there are loose threads in the fabric, too — I just know it. In my moments of doubt, I can hear Sam, feel him. He's urging me to take a leap of faith. *Come find me*, he's saying. *Pull the thread. Come dance with me.*

From: xk6c2-5765853262@gigs.craigslist.org
Date: December 20, 2016 at 3:24 p.m.
Subject: Re: ISO WIZARD FOR SPACE-TIME TRAVEL
To: Ion <e4825ab1386a3c06953a58ea13df71a0@
reply.craigslist.org>

Hello Wizard,

I am interested in your offer. Your credentials sound
impressive. Two of your colleagues have written with
very unreasonable demands. One requested that I
allow her to bring an iguana. The other wizard de-
manded a brick of gold as payment, and I don't have
any bricks of gold, though I suspect they were not
taking my ad seriously and were responding in jest. I
am actually serious about this.

Details: I need to get to the SilverCity Cinema at
approximately 7 p.m. on December 5, 2015, in order
to do the work necessary to prevent the catastrophe
of my partner's untimely death by an accidental overdose of illegal drugs on the 7th of December. I will
be bringing a copy of his obituary, pictures from his
funeral, and recent photos of our children to prove
that I have come from another dimension to save him
from himself. Also, I would like to bring the Death Star
cookie jar that houses his ashes so that we can spread
them together at the end of the Breakwater. If Sam
spreads his own ashes, I think he will really understand
how lucky he is to be alive in that dimension. He will
stop drinking like a river mouth and using whatever
other drugs he is taking, and we will live together into
old age as we were supposed to do here.

Completing this rescue will mean that my other self will have to be destroyed, but knowing myself, she would gladly sacrifice her experience of life to see a future without the kind of suffering she is having now.

Obviously, this all makes sense to you.

Write back. I need this, Wizard, and will give you the very best reference if you help me.

Yours truly,

-Elsie Jane

From: Ion <e4825ab1386a3c06953a58ea13df71a0@ reply.craigslist.org>

Date: December 21, 2016 at 3:49 p.m.

Subject: Re: ISO WIZARD FOR SPACE-TIME TRAVEL

To: xk6c2-5765853262@gigs.craigslist.org

Elsie Jane,

I am happy to inform you that this is indeed a noble goal and falls well within the boundaries of my code of ethics.

It is unfortunate that you did not have much luck with my colleagues, but it is in the nature of the field to attract all types of unsavoury characters, or at least many who are slightly unhinged. I may know the magus with the reptile obsession — you can trust me when I tell you that you dodged a bullet there.

My hardware can get us within close proximity of the SilverCity Cinema on the night in question, but I must warn you that if you were there to see a motion picture that in any way involved time travel, the whole plan may fall asunder. The Wormhole Lords have a tight grasp on clichés and a loose idea of what irony is and they've been known to deny passage to any circumstances that meet their nebulous criteria for these already nebulous concepts. As neither of us wants to get trapped in the netherworld between dimensions, I am sure you will be responsible and inform me if this is the case.

Also, my Quantum Spangler has a weight limit, so I may need to use my de-sizing spell on the Death Star cookie jar. My re-sizing spell works perfectly 99% of the time, so this shouldn't present a problem. I just firmly believe in making sure my clients are aware of all possible eventualities ahead of time.

Otherwise, your plan seems foolproof. Mice couldn't have laid it better. We are guaranteed success.

Regards,

-Ion

From: xk6c2-5765853262@gigs.craigslist.org
Date: December 22, 2016 at 3:01 a.m.
Subject: Re: ISO WIZARD FOR SPACE-TIME TRAVEL
To: Ion <e4825ab1386a3c06953a58ea13df71a0@reply.craigslist.org>

Dear Wizard,

I'm excited and grateful beyond measure. Thank you so much for taking me on as a client.

Can we please arrange an in-person meeting to discuss the plan?

-Elsie Jane

From: Ion <e4825ab1386a3c06953a58ea13df71a0@
reply.craigslist.org>
Date: December 24, 2016 at 11:19 p.m.
Subject: Re: ISO WIZARD FOR SPACE-TIME TRAVEL
To: xk6c2-5765853262@gigs.craigslist.org

Hello Elsie Jane,
Apologies for the tardy response.
    I've enjoyed our back and forth.
    I think I will take a time out from the role-playing
for now. Maybe we can connect after Christmas.
Best wishes,
-Paul

From: xk6c2-5765853262@gigs.craigslist.org
Date: December 25, 2016 at 4:30 p.m.
Subject: Re: ISO WIZARD FOR SPACE-TIME TRAVEL
To: Ion <e4825ab1386a3c06953a58ea13df71a0@
reply.craigslist.org>

Hello "Paul,"
You wouldn't be a professional if you didn't test my
faith in the science of quantum love. Wizard, please
be assured that I do believe in you. Please meet me
for lunch at Il Greco on December 27 at 12:30 p.m.
    I'll be wearing an orange scarf and a forlorn
expression.
Sincerely,
-Elsie

From: Ion <e4825ab1386a3c06953a58ea13df71a0@
reply.craigslist.org>
Date: December 26, 2016 at 7:03 a.m.
Subject: Re: ISO WIZARD FOR SPACE-TIME TRAVEL
To: xk6c2-5765853262@gigs.craigslist.org

I'm not meeting with you. I'm busy with the holidays
now. It was good fun, though.
Good luck.
-Paul

From: xk6c2-5765853262@gigs.craigslist.org
Date: December 26, 2016 at 2:37 p.m.
Subject: Re: ISO WIZARD FOR SPACE-TIME TRAVEL
To: Ion <e4825ab1386a3c06953a58ea13df71a0@
reply.craigslist.org>

Wizard,
Gotcha — we don't want the Wormhole Lords eaves-
dropping! ;)
    I will be there at 12:30 p.m. as planned. I so look
forward to meeting you. Would you mind giving me
a physical description, so I know who I'm looking
for?
-Elsie

From: Ion <e4825ab1386a3c06953a58ea13df71a0@
reply.craigslist.org>
Date: December 27, 2016 at 9:23 a.m.
Subject: Re: ISO WIZARD FOR SPACE-TIME TRAVEL
To: xk6c2-5765853262@gigs.craigslist.org

I won't be there, but enjoy your lunch.
-Paul

From: xk6c2-5765853262@gigs.craigslist.org
Date: December 27, 2016 at 11:49 p.m.
Subject: Re: ISO WIZARD FOR SPACE-TIME TRAVEL
To: Ion <e4825ab1386a3c06953a58ea13df71a0@
reply.craigslist.org>

Hi Wizard,
I can't say I'm not a bit hurt that you didn't show up
today. I waited for nearly two hours and paid for a
babysitter. Perhaps we could discuss the equivalent
of my time and cost of my meals being deducted
from your final invoice?

I'm still more than willing to work with you, as I am
truly impressed with your credentials. I hope you are
having a wonderful holiday!
-Elsie

From: Ion <e4825ab1386a3c06953a58ea13df71a0@
reply.craigslist.org>
Date: December 28, 2016 at 4:50 p.m.
Subject: Re: ISO WIZARD FOR SPACE-TIME TRAVEL
To: xk6c2-5765853262@gigs.craigslist.org

I think it's a bit weird that part of this game for you
involves posing as a grieving woman. It's not clever. I
do hope you had a good Christmas, though.

   Get some help?

-Paul

From: xk6c2-5765853262@gigs.craigslist.org
Date: December 28, 2016 at 11:34 p.m.
Subject: Re: ISO WIZARD FOR SPACE-TIME TRAVEL
To: Ion <e4825ab1386a3c06953a58ea13df71a0@
reply.craigslist.org>

Dear Wizard,

I can assure you I don't think I'm clever in any way.
This is not a joke. If I've offended you, I hope you will
forgive me. I'll be at Il Greco again tomorrow at 1 p.m.

   See you there :)

-Elsie

From: xk6c2-5765853262@gigs.craigslist.org

Date: December 29, 2016 at 3:19 p.m.

Subject: Re: ISO WIZARD FOR SPACE-TIME TRAVEL

To: Ion <e4825ab1386a3c06953a58ea13df71a0@
reply.craigslist.org>

Wizard,

You didn't show up again. I waited for two hours this
time. I thought it was a test, that you wanted me to
demonstrate my faith in the quantum-jumping process in order to know it was safe to move forward,
and that I can be trusted. I feel a little foolish now.

I will continue my search for another wizard.

Sincerest regards,

-Elsie

TWENTY-FIVE

I KNOW THIS WIZARD THING SEEMS LIKE AN ESCAPist fantasy, but it's not. I'm in that part of the movie where everything I've ever known is irrelevant, where this world has more possibility than what I can touch and see.

It's New Year's Eve. I am home with my kids, watching Benji make a tower out of blocks. He is so careful and so focused in this endeavour, his chubby little fingers struggling to bring the vision in his mind to life. Every time the tower falls, he cries out in frustration, but then he begins again, one block on top of another until it's twelve high and wobbly and clearly unable to bear the weight of one more block. I can see it, the inevitable collapse, but he can't.

Lark is drawing at the table. Flowers with lovely, freckled petals, three of them. She has written *Flower Family* at the bottom of the page.

I made chicken with rice and vegetables tonight. It felt like an extraordinary accomplishment. The step-by-step process of creating a meal has been too confounding for me to succeed at for over a year now. I've ruined all but two of my pots and pans by leaving boiling or frying things on the stove until the fire alarm went off. My kids have learned to expect frozen entrees, takeout, things that can be warmed from a can. But tonight, I did it: I made dinner, and then we sat around the table in our quiet little trio and ate together.

·It's the kids' bedtime now. I read *Red Is Best* to Benji for the four-hundredth time, and then Lark and I read *Diary of a Wimpy Kid* and play a few rounds of Would You Rather.

"You go first, Mama."

"Okay. Would you rather … be able to fly, or have the power to travel through space-time?"

"I would fly. What do you choose?"

"Travel through space-time."

"Okay, my turn. Would you rather … eat an old man's earwax, *or* … smell an old man's bum?"

"Smell the bum, definitely. What about you?"

"Neither."

"You can't do that. You have to choose!"

"I choose neither! You would smell an old man's bum!"

"No, I choose neither, too, then!"

"Sorry, you're not allowed. You love smelling old man bums!"

We both laugh until our guts ache.

Once the kids are asleep, I go upstairs and take thirty-two selfies on Snapchat, then settle into playing Candy Crush until I realize that midnight came and went some time ago. It's 2017, big fucking whoop. It's been four days since I heard from the Wizard and I'm starting to feel despondent and worry that he'll never write back and the game is over.

I check my email before I go to bed, just in case. Nothing.
Then I wake up at 4:10 a.m. and check again.

> From: Ion <e4825ab1386a3c06953a58ea13df71a0@
> ·reply.craigslist.org>
> Date: January 1, 2017 at 3:59 a.m.
> Subject: Re: ISO WIZARD FOR SPACE-TIME TRAVEL
> To: xk6c2-5765853262@gigs.craigslist.org
>
> Congratulations, Elsie Jane, and Happy New Year!
> You have passed with flying colours, my dear.
>   I will be in touch shortly with further instructions.
> Regards,
> -Ion

My stomach flips, my heart skips a beat, and I feel like flying. *And* space-time travelling.

I choose both.

With Ion's help, I'll be there, at the SilverCity Cinema in the
other timeline, ready to meet the other Elsie Jane at the exit. She'll
be stomping out to her car, all upset just like I was. I'll grab her,
drag her into the woods behind the theatre. I'm not sure how that
part will go, because I've never dragged anyone into the woods
before, so I'm counting on adrenalin. My only problem is that I
can't even kill a spider — I gather them so carefully in a cup and
put them outside — so mustering the resolve to commit homicide
is troublesome. And how will I even do it, anyway? Strangulation
seems barbaric, but then so does drowning. And beyond the obvious issue of needing to gift the other Elsie Jane a peaceful death
so that *I* can avoid PTSD, there will be empathy required, because being executed by your cosmic twin is the stuff of horror.

I don't want to look at her face while I do it, so smothering is probably best. The internet says smothering is an efficient method; you just have to wait a bit to ensure your victim doesn't start breathing again, but it should take only five minutes, max.

Once it's over with, I'll cover her with some leaves, grab her (my) keys and purse, and be back at the car just in time to catch Sam stumbling around the parking lot.

I can't wait to see him. I don't even care if he's drunk and sloppy, I'm not angry anymore. I'm going to do things differently this time.

Instead of driving home and telling Sam not to talk to me, I'll drive us to the Breakwater. We'll walk out to the end, sit in the alcove beneath the lighthouse. I'll open my backpack and show him all the things I've brought through the wormhole. The pictures from his funeral, the copy of his obituary. I'll let him hold the Death Star cookie jar, feel the weight of it. And I'll explain everything. *Everything.* How fragile it all is. *It doesn't have to end this way,* I'll tell him.

On our way back to the car, he'll stop and grab me, pull me close. We'll kiss. Hard like in the movies, salt wind whipping seaweed all around us.

Then we'll drive through Fairfield, admire the Christmas lights. I'll tell him about our first Christmas without him. How haunted it was. How Benji said, "Where Dada?" all morning.

On Quadra Street, I'll pull over in front of Sands Funeral Chapel. I'll tell him about his service. How bewildered his sister and parents and grandparents looked. How so many people showed up that they spilled into the lobby. How the kids had their hair combed and styled, how they wore their best shoes.

By the time we get home, he'll have sobered up. We'll pay
the babysitter, and then he'll tell *me* everything. What drugs
he was using, when he started. He'll answer all my questions. I
won't show disgust, or anger, or fear, only compassion.

And he'll say, "I'll do it. I'll go to treatment."

And he'll really mean it, and he'll really go.

TWENTY-SIX

I'VE BEEN VIBRATING NOW FOR TWO WEEKS, AND even though I haven't heard back from the Wizard despite several friendly prompts, I keep crying with human joy in the same way I cried during my pregnancies. At TV commercials, at Whitney Houston songs on the radio, at engagement and wedding photos that people post on Facebook. Something has shifted. It almost feels like gratitude. Not quite, but almost.

I have packed up my kitchen in order to pare things down for whoever is left to deal with things once I get the fuck out of here. I rolled all my extra coffee cups in newspaper, bubble-wrapped wineglasses and dessert plates, and packed them all in a box that I labelled neatly with a Sharpie. I went through the pantry and threw out all the expired cans. I scrubbed out the drawers and cupboards with vinegar and lavender oil, buffed the kitchen sink to a shine, and remembered how when Sam was alive, we would wash dishes together and I would give names to the colours that showed up in

the sunsets through the tall fir and arbutus trees. *Purplue.*
Orangink. Marmalade Fire.

I also packed my purple backpack. Inside, there are three
pairs of XL sexy underwear (I won't fit the other Elsie Jane's
size mediums anymore), the Death Star cookie jar, Sam's obituary, and a recent photo with all three kids feeding the ducks at
Beacon Hill Park: all items I will use to prove to the other Sam
that I am in fact an Interdimensional Being of Love, there to
rescue him from the depths of his addiction.

Of course, I've also been checking my email every hour on
the hour for my instructions from the Wizard. Nothing yet, but
I know beyond a shadow of a doubt that they're coming any day
now. The dead woman can't be a coincidence. She can't be. She is
me, I am her, and while it's a shame that the quantum-jumping
process was too much for her body to handle when she landed here,
I'm confident that I'll do better. I've been drinking protein shakes.

O

This afternoon I'm taking my kids for a walk around Rithet's
Bog in the low winter sun. There is frost on the ground and the
marshlands are frozen. Some of my mother's ashes are scattered
here (the rest are in an oak box on the top shelf of my bedroom
closet), because it was one of her favourite places. We ran here
together, she and I, nearly every day from the time I was thirteen until she met her second husband and decided that he was
a more suitable exercise companion.

"Your grandmother's spirit is here," I tell Lark. "It's in the
earth we're walking on, and in those cattails over there, and in
the roots of all the trees, and blowing in the wind."

"Well, that's creepy," she says.

Benji is running ahead. It's our first-ever walk without the stroller. His hair in the sun looks like a shiny new penny, and his little ears and nose are pink from the cold.

On the bridge over the creek, he finds a frozen baby bird that someone has placed on the railing.

"What's dat, Mama?"

"That's a baby bird."

"Why it's not flying?"

"Because it's dead. It's a dead bird."

"Oh. I throw it in the water?"

"No, don't touch it. We don't touch dead things."

"Where is the mama?"

"The mama bird? Oh, she's probably flying around somewhere, looking for her baby."

He is satisfied with this explanation and gallops on down the path.

I'm amazed that we've made it the entire way around the bog with no injuries or demands for me to carry him. Just as I register that amazement, though, he trips on a rock and goes flying into the brush. A branch has scraped the skin below his ear, and he's bleeding. I carry him the rest of the way, and for the first time in a very long time, the carrying doesn't feel like a burden. I smile at the other walkers we pass, who give me knowing looks about crying toddlers and smile back.

At home, I check my email to see if my instructions have arrived. Nothing yet, but the possibility fills me with energy. It's not just the idea of magic or quantum-jumping, or even of seeing Sam again. It's the prospect of escaping this hellscape of grief.

I make the kids dinner and take extra care to cut their grilled-cheese sandwiches into funny shapes. I slice fresh fruit, pour orange juice.

Look at you, suddenly being Martha Stewart, says my mother, and that's all she says — no other advice or reprimands.

Thank you, I say.

These kids, the ones in this timeline, are amazing. They're resilient, they'll be okay without me. I love them, of course. But let's face it, I've been a terrible mother since Sam died. They deserve better, and if I stay, I'll only screw them up by being a distant, sad mess for the rest of their lives. They'll be better off with my sister, who has an alive partner and isn't emotionally destroyed. I've deregistered all of my RRSPs, $115,000 worth. The money is sitting in an account I've set up for Lark, and just before I quantum-jump, I'll give my sister the PIN for the debit card. I've written her a letter with instructions as well, hidden in the freezer so Lark doesn't find it.

I'll be a much better mother for the kids in the other timeline, because I'll be back with Sam.

O

At midnight, I go outside and walk up to the top of the lawn, look down at the house. Sam and I had sex on this lawn, once, when the Old Lady was blasting opera in the wee hours of the morning. She normally played big band or the blues, but that night it was opera, robust and romantic and sweeping and sweet. Can you imagine fucking under the stars with opera floating through the air? Opera playing from the turntable of an actual old Italian? That's what we did. Afterward, we lay partially clothed on the prickles and moss. We marvelled at the oldness of the oak tree above us, how its branches looked like veins, or bronchioles, or hundreds of arthritic fingers reaching out for birds.

When I see him again, I'll remind him of that night.

TWENTY-SEVEN

I'M BACK TO WORK NOW. EVERYONE TELLS ME I'M
looking great.

"You look so rested. You have colour in your cheeks!"

"Oh my God, you look like a different person. *So* much
happier. Good for you for taking the time you needed!"

"Please don't take this the wrong way, but you seemed, like,
really unwell."

Nobody gives me frightened, pitying smiles; I don't cry in
the bathroom; and at lunch I go for walks with colleagues and
successfully talk about standard-variety person things. Real
estate prices, recipes, reality television. On the phone with
complainants, I'm warm and kind, professional and patient.
I do not get upset and sneak away for smokes with the security guards. If you saw me in the office these days, you'd never
know I was the same person as the haunted, bloated mess
of 2016. I arrive in the morning with a freshly washed face
and a clean tongue on account of having rediscovered soap

and toothbrushing. I banter, tease co-workers, crack jokes, and contribute strategically hilarious lines from *The Office* at team meetings, and everybody laughs, but not too hard, not too hard in the way people laugh when they know someone's fragile. They think I'm all better, that I've turned the corner, that I'm ready to embark on the next chapter of my life. I won't tell them about the dead woman and how it can't be a coincidence. They wouldn't believe that I'm her, that she is me. They wouldn't understand about Craigslist and the wizard and our quantum-jumping plan. If I told them the truth, they might worry.

O

It happens one dreary morning in February. I've just dropped the kids at school and daycare when my phone buzzes. I'm waiting in the Starbucks drive-through on my way to the office.

8:49 a.m. *Very short window to accomplish goal this morning. Meet me behind theatre @ 10 a.m. sharp. DO NOT BRING CELLPHONE.*

"Ma'am, your coffee?"

My hands are trembling. My whole being is trembling, but I take the coffee, and I tell the barista, "Thank you," and he says, "See ya later," and I say, "You'll never see me here again!"

8:50 a.m. *Wizard. Is it really you??*

"Ma'am, would you mind pulling forward so we can serve the next customer?"

I lurch ahead into a NO PARKING zone and my bumper scrapes over the sidewalk. I'm holding my phone and shaking it in the air right in front of my face, howling and laughing. How does he even have my phone number? I never gave it to him, did I? If I didn't, this feels all the more magical and urgent.

8:57 a.m. *Follow instructions. Don't be late.*

I have one hour to drive across town, grab my backpack and the Death Star cookie jar from home, and make it over to the theatre. It's going to be tight, so I'm forced to drive over the curb and across oncoming traffic to change directions. I speed all the way home. Starla is outside, vacuuming her truck.

"Hello, Starla! You're amazing at maintaining the cleanliness of your vehicle!"

"I ... thank you!"

My quantum-jumping supplies are in the foyer closet, so it's grab and go.

As I back out of the driveway, I honk at Starla and roll down my window.

"Have a nice life in this shitty timeline!"

On the drive to the theatre, I call my sister. We haven't spoken since the fight about Ada May, but I need to make arrangements for the kids.

"Hello?"

"It's me."

"Oh. Hi."

"I have something going on today, something urgent. I need someone to pick up my kids."

"Nice to hear from you. I'm fine, thanks."

"Great — can you get the kids for me?"

"Um, I guess?"

"And maybe keep them overnight?"

"I can get the kids, and I can probably keep them overnight. But why? What's going on?"

"It'll be longer than overnight."

"What?"

"Never mind, it's too complicated to explain. Do you have a pen? You have to write this down. I'll text it to you, but write it down now, too."

"I'm at work."

"Write it down!"

"Okay!"

"Zero four seven two nine nine. Write that down. It's a PIN: zero four seven two nine nine. Got it? It's a CIBC account in Lark's name and there is a letter for you with all the details under the chicken strips in my freezer."

"What would I need a letter for? Can you please tell me what's going on? You're scaring me."

"I have to go now. Thanks for getting the kids. They're done at three."

O

This whole last year will soon feel like a distant nightmare, a blip of bad juju in the grand scheme of things that I'll never need to worry about again. It will be a funny story we'll tell our grandchildren one day — how Grandma jumped through the multiverse to rescue Grandpa from a polysubstance overdose, how she loved him so much she was willing to risk becoming a corpse mistaken for a Jane Doe.

"Downtown Train" comes on the radio. It's the terrible Rod Stewart version, but I sing along anyway at the top of my lungs, and I don't even stop suddenly and pretend I wasn't singing at the red lights.

I've been on many trips in my life. I've been to France and I've been to Japan, I've been to Albania and Washington, D.C., but I've never traversed space-time through a wormhole with a wizard friend to rescue the love of my life.

I pull into the covered parking lot at exactly 10:00 a.m., grab the Death Star and my backpack, and run. Along the edge of the movie theatre, between the exterior walls of the library and the hockey arena, all the way to beyond where the park path winds along the forest's edge. I sprint through the woods, over stumps, under trees fallen by windstorms, until I make it to a clearing.

I recognize this place. It's the place from my dreams.

There's nobody here.

"Ion?"

I am the least patient person in the world, but I sit down on my backpack and wait without so much as a sigh. I don't even have my phone, just an analog watch.

Ten thirteen a.m.

It's kind of scary here.

It starts to rain, and I still wait. *This is fine. I'd wait all day and night to see Sam again. I will.*

Ten twenty-three a.m.

No sign of the wizard.

I hear rustling in the bush, but it's only a pair of fawns and their mother. It's really pouring now. I'm getting soaked, the wind is picking up and whistling through the trees, and with the blackness of the cloud cover, I'm feeling a little freaked out. Maybe it's another test, and he's been watching me this whole time?

"Ion? It's me, Elsie Jane! I came here, like you said! I'm here and I brought all the stuff!"

A branch cracks in the bush. I think I hear someone, but it's only the mother deer and her fawns again, this time cautiously stepping into the clearing.

"Yeah, that's fine, come on in," I say.

The mother deer freezes, and we lock eyes. Her two fawns are peeking at me, too, from under her belly.

I know this sounds weird, but I swear to God this deer is judging me. She looks imperious. Disappointed.

"You have no right to be critical of me," I say.

She just stares, her stupid ears flattened and dripping with rain.

"Oh, piss off," I tell her. "I have nothing to explain to you." But then ...

Oh my God.

It starts like a cold insect crawling up the back of my neck, and then it grows, crawls around, slaps me across the face, and jumps down my throat, floods my whole chest. Shame.

I'm not *abandoning* my kids, though. The ones in the other timeline, they'll still be *my* kids. Not the ones who've been with me through all of this, but the untroubled, younger versions of themselves. What's wrong with that?

That's okay, right?

Right?

The mother deer stares expectantly. *What kind of a mother would behave this way?* her eyes say.

"I am not my mother," I tell her.

She seems unconvinced by this comment. I can tell by her long, slow blink.

"I know that's what you're thinking. You're thinking I'm just like my mother, and her mother, too. You think me and my mother and Ada May are the same. You think I'm running away because life feels too hard and the connection is too painful."

Have you ever heard the sound a deer makes when they agree with you? That's the sound this mother deer makes, though she doesn't stop grooming her babe. It's a sound between a trumpet and a doggy toy. Staccato, definite.

The shame just sits there, in my chest and guts, throbbing.

The deer bows politely and takes her leave, her fawns bobbling along behind her.

Why didn't I wear socks? I didn't realize how cold it was until just now. My toes are raw inside my gumboots and I'm shivering turkey skin all over. The rain has soaked through the hood of my sweatshirt. It's dripping from my ears, running down my neck. I feel hungover, as if I've just woken up after a night of guzzling straight vodka, everything ridiculous and wrong and stupid about this whole plan throbbing like a headache.

"Well, the wizard isn't even coming, so I guess I'm not jumping through space-time anyway," I call after the deer, and to myself I mumble, "Because I'm a nice mom, like a deer mom."

But I'm not a nice mom. I'm a selfish mom. A solipsistic mom. The worst mom of all the moms in the multiverse.

I consider things very carefully. My mother's coldness after she was diagnosed with cancer, how cutting and critical she became. Ada May's impulse to fly away when the catastrophe of goodbye was looming, and how that impulse was born from wounds of my great-grandmother, taken from *her* mother at age five, one Winnipeg winter. I'm just the latest in this matryoshka doll of love and sorrow, standing now with a lot of rain in my face in the middle of a stupid urban forest, holding a Death Star cookie jar, threaded through and through with the same compulsions to detach, to dissociate, to flee.

And you know what conclusion I arrive at, having considered all of this very carefully?

Fuck it. Seriously, fuck it.

I don't have to be my mother, or Ada May, or any of the mothers before me who abandoned their children emotionally or physically or cosmically. I might be a grieving fool who tricked herself into believing that space-time wizards and quantum-jumping are real, but I don't have to be a running fool.

"I can be a mother who doesn't run away," I yell into the crying sky. And even though Ion the Wizard hasn't shown up and I guess I'm not quantum-jumping today or ever, I still feel like I'm making a choice.

I pick up my backpack, feeling triumphant, and start back toward the trail.

Ducking under a drooping spruce branch, I run headfirst and rather painfully into the chest of a mannequin.

"Ow, Jesus fuck."

I trip on a tree root, fall forward, land on my elbows in the mud. In my peripheral vision, the mannequin comes to life, moves toward me.

It is not a mannequin at all. It is a man. A very tall man.

"Hey, sorry about that. Y'good?"

He has a vintage Minolta camera hanging from his neck and an embarrassed, lopsided smile hanging from his face. "Elsie Jane," he says apologetically, offering me his hand.

I take it. He helps me up, and we stand there examining each other. He looks young, maybe twenty-five, thirty tops, and he has one wet ringlet in the middle of his forehead. Wild blue eyes, searching and kind.

I'm pissed.

"Have you been here this whole time?" I ask.

"I'm late. Sorry about that." An Irish lilt.

"It's fine." I sniff. "I'm just leaving, actually."

"I know, I heard you chatting with the deer."

"So you have been here. Where's your wizard hat and the Quantum Spangler?"

"Stolen. I was actually accosted on my way here by a roving band of time torque lurchers in the Starbucks loo."

I laugh.

"Sorry," he says, "I couldn't hold it. I had no idea they could crawl out of the toilet!"

"All right, that's enough," I say.

But now we're both laughing, and they are the laughs of absolute shared delight, the laughs of old jokes between old friends after too many beers. I laugh so hard that I have to put my hands on my knees to catch my breath. I laugh so hard I fart, and then we both laugh harder.

"You actually came here to be a wizard with me!" I shout through hysterical wheezing giggles. "And you're a handsome Irish stranger in the fucking forest, what the faaack*aahahaha*!"

I look up at him, hands still on my knees, my grin wide and genuine, and he raises his camera and snaps a picture.

"Don't take a picture of me, you fucking weirdo."

"Oh, *I'm* the fucking weirdo, am I?"

"Erase that."

"I can't, it's film."

"Oh God."

O

Ion pulls an old beach blanket from the trunk of his car, dries his hair and face, and offers it to me, and I wipe the smeared mud from my elbows. I text my sister, apologize for freaking her out, tell her I can pick up the kids after all. She responds immediately.

You scared the shit out of me. Was about to call police. Don't ever do that again. Not funny.

I'm sorry. For everything. Not just today.

I see the three dots moving and then disappearing, then moving again, but she doesn't respond.

O

Ion takes me for lunch at Il Greco. We talk about stuff. What's real, what's not. He loved my ad, he says, he had to play along, but did I really — but seriously — did I *really* think there was a chance he could be an actual wizard?

Yes, I tell him, of course I thought so. You don't know what I've been through, I tell him. He agrees that he does not. How old are you? I ask. Thirty-three, he says, tapping three fingers on the table twice. I imagine making out with him. It is an acceptable image.

His name is Paul, not Ion. Yes, he's from Ireland. No, he actually doesn't read much sci-fi. He's a movie buff, he says. He has weird taste, and he loved that movie *Safety Not Guaranteed*, which my ad reminded him of. I've never seen it, I tell him, and he says we should watch it sometime. I change the subject. These dolmades are dry, I say — anyway, what's your job? He's an arborist, not a wizard, ha ha, and yes, he does think trees can feel pain. I do, too, I tell him. Because I really do.

I tell him about Sam, my mom, my dad. He tells me about his sister and his mom, how they both died by suicide just a year apart, back in Ireland.

At two thirty, the restaurant is closing for its pre-dinner clean, the servers passive-aggressively flipping the chairs onto the tables all around us.

"I have to get my kids now," I say.

"Okay," he says. "Okay."

Paul asks me if I'll have lunch with him again one day.

"Sure," I say. Then, "Maybe."

O

Lark has been in a fight at school. She's sobbing when I pick her up. A boy pushed her off the monkey bars, and so she grabbed him by the hood of his coat and it ripped off.

"There's a note in my bag from the principal," she says, looking at her knees, her little chin quivering.

"You know what? I'm glad you ripped his coat."

Her eyes light up.

And now it's pizza for dinner, but fancy: on plates, at the table. Benji counts backward from ten while Lark sings an inappropriate song about butts from YouTube.

And now it's bath, stories, bed — the muscle memory of motherhood.

And now, with the kids asleep, I open my emails, find my favourite one, the best one, the email from Sam that I return to over and over:

From: Sam <Qbit_Sam@vergemail.com>

Date: February 9, 2013 at 11:39 p.m.

Subject: Library of Babel

To: Elsie J. <Elsiejane@vergemail.com>

I know a boy who likes you. Guess.

I can't wait to fly home. It's been a fun confer-ence, but I can't wait to get on that plane and home to you and our bed.

Hey, I know you tease me about getting too sappy. You can make fun of me if you want to, I don't mind. I appreciate that you put up with it, my tendency to interrogate the edges of things to find softness. I ap-preciate that you let me, even when it's silly or over the top. But this. This isn't silly, okay? This is serious.

Have you heard of "The Library of Babel," of Borges? I'm not sure we've discussed it before. It's his conception of the universe as a library, an infin-ite super-geometrical structure of space-time where every possible version of every story is contained in its shelves.

Initially, the idea might seem devoid of passion or humanity, because infinity, too, is theoretical. But listen, listen. It holds, within it, the book of you and me. I imagine a dream version of myself in that li-brary, haunting its shelves, running up ladders that expand in every direction. And finally, finding it. Our book. The story of you and me. And finding a quiet corner, and settling down to read. Devouring every word, enraptured, at peace, reading of our first, and last, embraces.

What will you look like when you're really old?
I think I'll find out. Is it strange that I want to do it
now, right now, and fast-forward our lives just for the
pleasure of seeing all of you at once? Your eyes, I
know, will look the same. I wonder about all they'll
have seen. It puts a smile on my face to think about.
Like this: :)
We better take care of each other, and ourselves,
so we can find out what old age looks like.
I love you. Completely. The boy is me.
Good night, Elsie.

Like every other night, I read it many times. Like every other night, I cry. But tonight, for the first time, I do something I've never done before. I hit *Reply*.

From: Elsie J. <Elsiejane@vergemail.com>
Date: February 9, 2017 at 11:39 p.m.
Subject: Re: Library of Babel
To: Sam <Qbit_Sam@vergemail.com>

Dear Sam,
There's no wizard coming for me, no wormhole that
I can jump through to escape the configurations of
love and pain I arrived in somehow because of us.
Maybe there is no unsullied universe on the other side
of anywhere.
The kids are so big. They're so beautiful and an-
noying and so great. I wish you could see them.
My sister and I are fighting. I've been selfish and
unhinged since you died. Seriously selfish, seriously

unhinged. I smashed a lot of the plates your mom bought us.

I wonder if you'd even recognize me if you met me now. I know I'd recognize you anywhere, but I don't think you'd recognize me if you walked in and saw me sitting here, tonight. Thirty pounds fatter, dark circles under my eyes. I look so old and so sad and it's all your fault. Probably no one will ever love me again.

If the roles were reversed and it was me who died, I bet you'd do a better job than I've been doing. I suck at this. I suck at grieving, and the worst part is that I've had enough practice that I should be really good at it by now. If it was you, I bet you would have taken the kids to Disneyland for a year or something. I can still barely manage the park.

I think I'm jealous of you. It's completely unjust that you don't have to answer any questions. You just get to *poof!* disappear, no accountability, and everybody else has to deal with the fallout. You really got off the hook in all of this, you know that?

On a daily basis, there are at least three moments where I think, *I hope I get extinguished today.* Like, *I hope today's the day I get T-boned by a semi or crushed by an anvil.* A passive, merciful end, no planning or energy required. And then I think about how you didn't know you were going to die, and I wonder if you ever had these fantasies of extinguishment. I wonder a lot about your thoughts. *What was he thinking when ...*

I know you sought oblivion, but I don't get why. We had so much together here. We had everything, actually — all the blissful, normal, stupid luckiness in the world.

I read your old emails so often that I've pretty much got them all memorized. This one that I'm replying to is my favourite. Every time I read it, I think, really? Did he really write this to me? How could it be that someone could love me so much, and I could love them so much back?

Maybe I'll keep emailing you. I have a lot to tell you. Like how I fucked Saul Waters, *Literary Shit Disturber*. Joyfully, spitefully. I was so fucking lonely and mad at you. I don't regret it.

I've been on a lot of terrible internet dates. Leonard Cohen died. I got in a fight with a beautiful blond in a fast-food play area. Ada May died. An owl came.

Hey, remember when we watched Trump descend on that golden escalator and you laughed so hard and said it was all a publicity stunt and he'd never be president?

You would seriously not believe all the shit that's happened since you left. Like today, even. I met an Irishman in the forest today. He was pretending to be a wizard. It's a funny story — you would laugh. I'm tired, so I'll write you more tomorrow night, k?

Love you.

-Elsie Jane

END

ACKNOWLEDGEMENTS

Erin Clyburn is an amazing literary agent and an outstanding human being. Thank you for believing in this book, championing it, and ushering it into existence.

Thank you to Dundurn Press and the Rare Machines team: Kwame Scott Fraser, Russell Smith, Erin Pinksen, Laura Boyle, Maria Zuppardi, Alyssa Boyden. Russell, thank you for taking a chance on an unknown writer and guiding me through the editing process with wit, warmth, and encouragement. Laura, thank you for the gorgeous cover. Massive thanks to editor Vicky Bell for your incredibly skilled copy edits, and to Erin Pinksen for your wonderful eye for detail. I am still pinching myself at getting to work with such an amazing group of professionals.

Eythan Slootweg saw a silly ad on Craigslist in 2016 and decided to respond. I tracked him down on Facebook in 2022, apologized for the unsolicited message from a stranger, and asked if he happened to respond to a Craiglist ad back in 2016 about a space-time wizard. "Yeah, that sounds like something I'd do," he replied. Eythan, thank you for allowing me to include your hilarious responses in the book, and thanks for our friendship. You're a brilliant writer and I can't wait to read your first novel.

Laura and Peter Walton and Debbie and Erik Noesgaard are my lovely in-laws and grandparents to my kids. Thank you for welcoming me into your family circle, and thank you for keeping me and parenting me. Thank you for your grace, love, and care. I am truly lucky to be swimming through this life with all of you, even through many painful waters.

Thank you to Lisa Noesgaard, my friend and sister-in-law. For that extremely weird trip to Garbage Beach. For your excellent taste in music and films. For introducing JP to cult horror, terrifying midway rides, gleeful and determined adventure-seeking, and to having his mental models of the universe explored and revelled in (and challenged when necessary). Thank you for carrying and sharing stories that span a lifetime, even as you carry an impossibly heavy loss in your flesh, blood, and memory.

Thank you to my sister, Jessica Steeves, for your suggestions, for your searching and sensitive heart, for allowing me to spin stories out of truly painful experiences. You are always my first reader and my partner in art, music, and motherhood. We go to zee ice cream now.

Thank you to my parents, who have both crossed Ye Olde Rainbow Bridge and are frolicking in heaven with many goats, good food, good friends, and good beer. May you forgive each other. To my father, Daryl Wakelyn, whose storytelling and humour I will always strive to emulate, thank you for always holding me in such high regard even when I definitely didn't earn or deserve it, and for sharing your amazing record and book collections with me. To my mother, Laurel Doersam, whose passion and intensity I strive and regularly fail to un-mirror, thanks for having my back for a solid 75 percent of our time together. Good enough. Thank you for modelling that mothers are allowed to be flawed, complicated beings with their own dreams. I didn't always get that. I get it now.

Thanks to my auntie Dawn Jones, who has loved and sup-ported me unconditionally my whole life.

Josh Szczepanowski, Betty-Ann Lampman, and Jenny Amber, all busy and brilliant artists and makers themselves, each took the time to read chaotic early drafts and gave me candid, generous feedback. Thank you so much.

Huge thanks to Jill Margo, an incredible writer who is also a gifted developmental editor, coach, and mentor. How you do all that?

Tove Shea is my witch wife whose magic spells and emo-tional poetics astound me on the daily. Thanks for being weird with me. I couldn't do anything without you.

David Chenery is a prolific songwriter whose genius I see reflected in our daughter's ways of being in the world. Thanks for being a great friend and co-parent.

Thanks to my beloved childhood friends, Kimberly Wood, Keeley Teuber, and Timothy Francis. I wouldn't be the me I am today without you (for better or worse). I can't wait to get old and sit on benches and drink milk with each of you, separately.

Kris Westendorp, Kelly Hobson, Dwayne Strohm, Shannon Strohm, Amanda Prenger, Sarah Rhude, J. McLaughlin, David P. Smith, Evan Pine, you have all inspired and encouraged me in some kind of way over the years. Thank you.

Carlin Dunsmoor-Farley, Shenoa Tobin, Emma Chenery, Kelly Finerty, Chrystine Green, Lise Berube, Jay Dunphy,

Masha Planedin, Dr. Nickolas J. Cherwinksi, Kate Baker, James Wood, Sonya Gracey, Emily Lindsay, Juliet Rice, Danielle Davis, Keith and Suzanne Noesgaard, and all my kindred spirits in the *Honestly* circle, thanks for being part of my life.

I'm grateful for the amazing teachers I've had over the years who encouraged me to write and keep writing. Mrs. Senior was my grade 1 teacher who let me make storybooks instead of forcing me to participate in class. Mr. McLeod was my grade 6 and 7 teacher who was inspiring and adventurous, read us great books, and took us cycling across tiny islands and camping in remote lagoons. Sorry I ruined Carrington Bay by getting my leg crushed by that beach log.

I know I join a chorus of gratitude for the incomparable poet and novelist Terence Young, who also happens to be the best teacher of writing and English in the universe. Thank you for everything, Terence.

Thanks to my GP, Dr. Anna Mason, a truly gifted physician. You have seen me through *allll* the shit with so much skill, compassion, and kindness.

Thanks to Daemon Baker, a man of great integrity who insists that love can be steady and calm, and whose actions reflect his words. I couldn't have finished this book without you.

Thank you to my children. You are forces of nature with tender hearts and curious minds, and I can't wait to see how you each change the world. I love you infinity much. Thanks for putting up with my writing, and for reminding me that I must also acknowledge cats. Thanks, cats, you guys are hilarious.

Thank you to Kris. For sharing all your gifts, and for the gifts you've left behind. Knowing you was a highlight in many lives, and being known by you was a miracle in mine.

ABOUT THE AUTHOR

Chelsea Wakelyn is a writer and musician. Born and raised on Vancouver Island, she grew up on the shores of Robinson Lake in Black Creek. She was an annoying, feral child, always covered in mud and scrapes and bruises. This was considered normal in the '80s, and she ran and swam with a pack of others like her. She and her siblings raised five pet goats (Mary, Gorby, Boris, Faleen, and Bubba) who were sadly re-homed when her parents divorced. Chelsea has worked the shirt press at a dry cleaner, baked oversized muffins and scones as a baker/barista, sold classified ad space at a weekly tabloid, and played the glockenspiel in a death-country band called The Lonesome Valley Singers. She lives in Nanaimo with her family. This is her first novel.